THREE OF A KIND

by the same author

THEFT
MRS CALIBAN
BINSTEAD'S SAFARI

RACHEL INGALLS

Three of a Kind

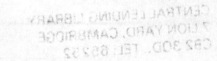

faber and faber
LONDON · BOSTON

First published in 1985
by Faber and Faber Limited
3 Queen Square London WC1N 3AU

Phototypeset by Wilmaset Birkenhead Merseyside
Printed in Great Britain by
Robert Hartnoll & Co. Ltd. Bodmin Cornwall

British Library Cataloguing in Publication Data

Ingalls, Rachel
Three of a kind,
I. Title
813'.54[F]   PS3559.N38

ISBN 0–571–13606–0

CONTENTS

I SEE A LONG JOURNEY

Flora had met James when she was going out with his younger brother, Edward. She'd been crazy about Edward, who even then had had a reputation for wildness where girls were concerned. She'd been eighteen, Edward nineteen. James was thirty-one.

She'd liked him straight away. He was easy in talking to her: relaxed and completely open, as if they'd known each other a long time. In fact, in a way she did know him already – not just through Edward, but from her older sister, Elizabeth, who had gone out with him for about two months a few years before. He had had many girlfriends and mistresses, naturally. He was agreeable and amusing, well-known everywhere and well-liked. He was also the most important of the heirs.

When he proposed to her, she thought her decision over carefully. She wasn't in love with him but she couldn't think of any reason why she should turn him down. He'd become such a good friend that she felt they were already related.

After the marriage, Edward changed along with everything else. The barriers came up all around her. Where once, on the outside, she had felt shut out of their exclusive family, now – on the inside – she was debarred from the rest of the world.

There had been a time at the beginning when she had fought. If it hadn't been for the money, she might have succeeded. Their quarrels, misunderstandings and jealousies were like those of other families. And she was like other girls who marry into a group of powerful personalities. She was tugged in different directions by all of them. They expected things of her. They criticized her. They tried to train and educate her. When she was pregnant for the first time, and when she had the child, they told her what she was doing wrong.

9

But that was the stage at which she found her own strength: she clung to the child and wouldn't let them near it. They had to make concessions. It was the first grandchild and a boy. She was sitting pretty. She could take her mother-in-law up on a point in conversation and make her back down.

Shortly after the birth a lot of pressure was taken off her anyway; Edward formed a liaison with a girl who sang in a nightclub. He was thinking of marrying her, he said. He wanted to introduce her to his parents – her name was Lula. His mother hit the roof about it. She described the girl as 'an unfortunate creature: some sort of half-breed, I believe'. Quarrels exploded over the breakfast table, down in the library, out in the garden. In the kitchen, of course, they were laughing.

She met Lula. Edward took them both out to lunch. Flora wasn't nervous about it: she even tried to put the other woman at her ease by saying that she too had once been an outsider to the family. But Lula wasn't going to accept anyone's sympathy. She put on a performance, talked loudly, looking around at the other people in the restaurant, pinched Edward under the table and went out of her way to throw as many dirty words as possible into every sentence. Then she stood up abruptly, declared that it had been so very, very nice but she had to run along now, tugged Edward by the hair and left.

'She isn't like that,' he said.

'You don't have to tell me. I could see. She'll be all right when we get together next time.'

'She really isn't like that.'

'I know. I told you – I recognize the camouflage. I liked her fine.'

'I think you made her feel unsure.'

'And I'm the easy one. Wait till she meets the others. She'll have her work cut out for her.'

'They gave you a rough time, I guess.'

'It's all right. That's over now.'

'It's mainly Mother.'

'It's the whole deal.'

'But things are okay between you and James?'

'Oh, yes,' she said. 'But we're in the thick of everything. If you and I had married, we could have escaped together.'

'But we didn't love each other,' he said matter-of-factly. It upset her to hear him say it. Someone should love her. Even her children – they needed her, but she was the one who did the loving.

'Besides,' he told her, 'I'm not sure that I want to escape. Even if it were possible. And I don't think it is.'

'It's always possible if you don't have children.'

He said, 'It's the price of having quarterly cheques and dividends, never having to work for it. Think of the way most people live. Working in a factory – could you stand it?'

'Maybe it wouldn't be so bad. If you were with somebody you loved.'

'Love doesn't survive much poverty. Unless you're really right down at the bottom and don't have anything else.'

Was it true? If she and her husband were lost and wandering in the desert, maybe he'd trade her for a horse or a camel, because he could always get another wife and have more children by the new one. It couldn't be true.

'I'm sure it would,' she said.

'From the pinnacle, looking down,' he told her, 'you get that romantic blur. Wouldn't it be nice in a little country cottage with only the birds and the running streams? It's the Marie Antoinette complex.'

And at another time he'd said, 'Love is a luxury for us. If I were on a desert island with the soulmate of all time, I'd still have the feeling that I'd ducked out. I guess it's what they used to call "duty".'

'There are plenty of others to take over the duties,' she'd told him.

'And they'd all think: *he wasn't up to it*. And they'd be right.'

It took two years for the family to wean Edward away from Lula. Then they set him up with a suitable bride, an Irish heiress named Anna-Louise, whose family was half-German

11

on the mother's side. One of Anna-Louise's greatest assets was that she was a superb horsewoman. Flora liked her. The boys' father, the old man, thought she was wonderful. His wife realized too late that Anna-Louise was a strong character, not to be bullied. Flora was let off the hook. She didn't allow her mother-in-law to take out on her or her children any of the failures and frustrations she had with Anna-Louise. She put her foot down. And eventually her mother-in-law came to her to seek an ally, to complain and to ask for advice. Flora listened and held her peace. She was learning.

James was the one who helped her. He guided her through her mistakes; he was the first person in her life to be able to teach her that mistakes are actually the best method of learning and that it's impossible to learn without at least some of them. He warned her about things she would have to know, strangers she was going to meet. She was grateful. But she also saw that he was part of the network and that all his actions, though well-meant, were aimed at making her just like the rest of them, whether she wanted to be or not.

It always came down to the question of money. The money made the difference. They were one of the richest families on the Eastern seaboard. Flora's own parents were from nice, substantial backgrounds; they'd had their houses and companies and clubs, and belonged to the right places when it had still been worth keeping up with that sort of thing.

She'd known people who knew the cousins, who gave parties at which she would be acceptable – that was how she had met Edward. Everyone knew about them. Everyone recognized their pictures in the papers. To marry into their ranks was like marrying into royalty, and a royalty that never had to worry about its revenues.

Her marriage had also changed her own relatives irrevocably. It was as though they had lost their thoughts and wishes; they had become hangers-on. They name-dropped with everyone, they could no longer talk about anything except the last time they'd seen James or Edward or – best of all – the old man.

They were all corrupted. One early summer afternoon Flora sat playing cards with James and Edward and her sister, Elizabeth, who had married a cousin of the family and thus, paradoxically, become less close.

Flora thought about the four of them, what they were doing with the time they had. All except for James were still in their twenties and they were like robots attached to a master-computer – they had no ideas, no lives. They were simply parts of a machine.

She wondered whether James and Elizabeth had slept together long ago, before she had become engaged to him, and thought they probably had. An exhaustion came over her: the artificial weariness enforced upon someone who has many capabilities and is consistently prevented from using any of them.

The doctors called it depression. She worked on her tennis, went swimming three times a week, and helped to organize charity fund-raising events. She made progress. Now she was an elegant young matron in magazine pictures, not the messy-haired girl who had run shrieking down the hallway from her mother-in-law's room as she held her squealing baby in one arm and then slammed and locked the door after her. She would never again stay behind a locked door, threatening to cut her throat, to go to the newspapers, to get a divorce. James had stood on the other side of the door and talked to her for five hours until she'd given in.

And now they had their own happy family together and she moved through the round of public and domestic duties as calmly and gracefully as a swan on the water. But the serenity of her face was like the visible after-effect of an illness she had survived; or like a symptom of the death that was to follow.

* * *

James thought they should take their holiday in a spot more remote than the ones they usually chose in the winter. He was fed up with being hounded by reporters and photographers.

13

And she was nervous about the children all the time. The house had always received a large quantity of anonymous mail and more than the average number of unpleasant telephone cranks. Now they were being persecuted not just because of their wealth, but because it was the fashion. Every day you could read in the papers about 'copy cat' crimes – acts of violence committed in imitation of something the perpetrators had seen on television or in the headlines of the very publication you had in your hand. If there had been a hoax call about a bomb at some large public building, it was fairly certain that the family secretaries would be kept busy with their share of telephone threats in the next few days. Everyone in the house was on speaking terms with at least ten policemen. There had been many crises over the years. They counted on the police, although James's mother, and his sister Margaret's ex-husband too, said they sometimes thought that most of the information these nuts and maniacs found out about them came straight from the police themselves.

Anna-Louise's entry into the family had brought further complications, adding an interest for the Irish connections on all sides. Anna-Louise herself wasn't afraid. She wasn't in any case the sort of woman who worried, but on top of that, her children hadn't been put in danger yet, whereas Margaret's had: her daughter, Amy, was once almost spirited away by a gang of kidnappers. 'Fortunately,' Margaret told friends later, 'they got the cook's niece instead. She was standing out at the side of the back drive, and it just shows how dumb these people are: it was Sunday and she was wearing a little hat, white gloves, a pink organdie dress and Mary Janes. If they'd known anything about Amy, they'd have realized she wouldn't be caught dead in a get-up like that. As a matter of fact, at that time of day on a Sunday, she'd be in her jeans, helping MacDonald in the greenhouses.'

They had paid handsomely to get the niece back; good cooks weren't easy to find. But they'd cooperated with the police, which they wouldn't have dared to do if Amy herself had been the victim: it would have been too big a risk, even though in

14

that particular case it had worked and they had caught the three men and rescued the girl. Flora later began to think it would have been better for the niece not to have lived through the capture; she started to crack up afterwards and developed a bitter enmity towards Amy, who, she told everybody, ought to have been the one to be seized.

The incident had taken place when Flora was in the beginning months of her second pregnancy. It brought home to her how difficult it was to escape the family destiny: even the children were dragged into it. And though it was only one of the many frightening, uncomfortable or calamitous events from the background of her first few years of marriage, it was the one that turned her into a woman who fretted about the future and who, especially, feared for the safety of her children. James tried to soothe her. On the other hand, his friend and chauffeur, Michael, who kept telling her everything would be all right, seemed at the same time to approve of the fact that she worried. She thought he felt it was a proof that she was a good mother.

'If we go too far away,' she said to James, 'the children – '

'We'll have telephones and telegraphs, and an airport nearby. It isn't any worse than if we were going to California for the weekend.'

'But it's so far away.'

He asked, 'What could we do, even here, if anything happened?' The question was meant to mollify, but it scared her even more.

'The doctor says you need a rest,' he insisted. She agreed with that. It seemed odd that a woman should live in a house as large as a castle, with nothing to do all day but easy, pleasant tasks, and still need a rest. But it was true.

'Michael will be with us,' he added.

That, finally, convinced her. If Michael came along, nothing bad could happen, either at home or abroad. She was distrustful of even the smallest disruption to her life, but she wanted to go. And she would be relieved to get away from the menace of all the unknown thousands who hated her without even having met her.

15

You couldn't be free, ever. And if you were rich, you were actually less often free than other people. You were recognized. The spotlight was on you. Strangers sent you accusations, threats and obscene letters. And what had you done to them? Nothing. Even the nice people were falsified by the ideas they had of your life; those who didn't threaten, begged. Everyone wanted money and most of them felt no shame at demanding it outright. They were sure they deserved it, so they had to have it. It didn't matter who gave it to them.

She too had been altered, of course. She had made her compromises and settled down. Of all the people connected with the family only Michael, she felt, had kept his innocence. His loyalty was like the trust of a child. When he drove her into town to shop, when they said hello or goodbye, she thought how wonderful it would be to put her arms around him, to have him put his arms around her. She was touched and delighted by all his qualities, even at the times when she'd seen him thwarted or frustrated and noticed how he went white and red very quickly.

'All right,' she said. 'If Michael comes too.'

'Of course,' James told her. 'I wouldn't be without him. There's a good hotel we can stay at. I don't think you'll need a maid.'

'I don't want a maid. I just want to be able to phone home twice a day to check if everything's all right.'

'Everything's going to be fine. You know, sometimes kids can get sick of their parents. It won't do them any harm to miss us for a week or two.'

'Two?'

'Well, if we don't make it at least two, half the trip's going to be spent in the plane, or recovering from jet-lag.'

* * *

They had parties to say goodbye: the friends' party, the relatives', and one birthday party for Margaret's youngest child, which coincided with a garden club meeting. Flora's mother-in-law directed the gloved and hatted ladies around flowerbeds that were to be mentioned in the yearly catalogue. Her father-in-law put in a brief appearance at the far end of the Italian gardens, shook hands with a few of the women and came back to the house, where he stayed for quite a while looking with delectation at the children digging into their ice cream and cake. Flora smiled at him across the table. She got along well with him, as did all his daughters-in-law, though Anna-Louise was his favourite. His own daughters had less of his benevolence, especially Margaret, whose whole life had been, and was still, lived in the always unsuccessful effort to gain from him the admiration he gave so freely to others. That was one of the family tragedies that Flora could see clearly. No one ever said anything about it and she'd assumed from the beginning that, having grown up with it, they'd never noticed. It was simply one more truth that had become acceptable by being ritualized.

The birthday room was filled with shouts and shrieks. Food was smeared, thrown and used to make decorations. One boy had built a palace of cakes and candies on his plate. There were children of industrialists, oil millionaires, ambassadors, bankers and heads of state; but they looked just like any other children, grabbing each other's paper hats while one of them was sick on the rug.

Michael too was looking on. He was enjoying himself, but he was there to work. He watched with a professional, noting glance. If anything went wrong, he was there to stop it. His presence made Flora feel safe and happy. She began to look forward to the trip.

The next evening, it was the grown-ups' turn to be sick on the rug. Five of their guests had to stay over for the weekend. On Monday morning Flora and James left for the airport.

At first she'd wanted to take hundreds of photographs with her. She'd started looking through the albums and every few pages taking one or two out; then it was every other page. Finally she had a fistful of pictures, a pile as thick as a

17

doorstop. James chose twelve, shoved the others into a drawer and told her they had to hurry now.

The children waved and smiled, their nurse cried. 'I wish she wouldn't do that,' Flora said in the car. 'Bursting into tears all the time.'

'Just a nervous habit,' he told her. 'It doesn't seem to affect the kids. They're a pretty hard-bitten bunch.' He clasped his hand over hers, over the new ring he had given her the night before. She tried to put everything out of her mind, not to feel apprehensive about the plane flight.

They were at the airport with plenty of time to spare, so he took her arm and led her to the duty-free perfume, which didn't interest her.

'There's a bookstore,' she said.

'All right.'

They browsed through thrillers, war stories, romantic novels and books that claimed to tell people how society was being run and what the statistics about it proved.

They became separated. The first James knew of it was when he heard her laugh coming from the other side of the shop and saw her turn, looking for him. She was holding a large magazine.

'Come look,' she called. The magazine appeared to be some kind of colouring book for children. There was a whole shelf full of the things. After the paper people in the drawings were coloured and cut free, you snipped out the pictures of their clothes and pushed the tabs down over the shoulders of the dolls.

'Aren't they wonderful?' she said. 'Look. This one's called "Great Women Paper Dolls". It's got all kinds of . . . Jane Austen, Lady Murasaki, Pavlova. Look at the one of Beatrix Potter: she's got a puppy in her arms when she's in her fancy dress, but underneath it's a rabbit. And – '

'These are pretty good,' he said. He'd discovered the ones for boys: history, warfare, exploration. 'As a matter of fact, the text to these things is of a very high standard. Too high for a colouring book.'

18

'Paper doll books.'

'You've got to colour them before you cut them out. But anybody who could understand the information would be too old to want one. You wonder who they're aimed at.'

'At precocious children like ours, of course. They'll think they're hysterical. We can send them these. Paper dolls of Napoleon and Socrates. Look, it says here: if I don't see my favourite great woman, I may find her in the book called "Infamous Women Paper Dolls". Oh James, help me look for that one.'

'Flora,' he said, 'the children are here. We're the ones who are supposed to be going away.'

'Yes, but we can send them right now, from the airport. Aren't they funny? Look. Infamous Women – how gorgeous. Catherine di Medici, Semiramis. And in the other one – here: an extra dress for Madame de Pompadour; the only woman to get two dresses. Isn't that nice? She'd have appreciated that.'

She was winding herself up to the point where at any moment her eyes would fill with tears. He said, 'Who's that one? Looks like she got handed the castor oil instead of the free champagne.'

'Eadburga.'

'Never heard of her.'

'It says she was at her worst around 802. Please, James. We can leave some money with the cashier.'

'Anything to get you out of this place,' he told her.

After they'd installed themselves in their seats and were up in the air, he said, 'What was the difference between the great and the infamous?'

'The great were artists and heroic workers for mankind,' she said. 'The infamous were the ones in a position of power.'

The speed of her reply took him by surprise. He couldn't remember if it might have been true. Florence Nightingale, he recalled, had figured among the greats; Amelia Earhart, too. But there must also have been a ruler of some sort:

19

Elizabeth I, maybe? Surely Queen Victoria had been in the book of good ones. And Eleanor of Aquitaine had been on a page fairly near that. He was still thinking about the question after Flora had already fallen asleep.

* * *

They arrived in an air-conditioned airport much like any other, were driven away in limousines with smoked-glass windows and were deposited at their hotel, where they took showers and slept. The first thing they did when they woke up was to telephone home. They didn't really look at anything until the next day.

They walked out of the marble-pillared hotel entrance arm in arm and blinked into the sun. They were still turned around in time. Already Flora was thinking about an afternoon nap. They looked to the left and to the right, and then at each other. James smiled and Flora pressed his arm. The trip had been a good idea.

They strolled slowly forward past the large, glittering shops that sold luxury goods. You could have a set of matching jade carvings packed and sent, jewellery designed for you, clothes tailored and completed in hours. James said, 'We can do all that later.' Flora stopped in front of a window display of jade fruit. She said, 'It's probably better to get it over with.'

They stood talking about it: whether they'd leave the presents till later and go enjoy themselves, or whether they ought to get rid of the duties first, so as not to have them hanging over their heads for two weeks. Michael waited a few feet to the side, watching, as usual, without seeming to.

They decided to do the difficult presents first – the ones that demanded no thought but were simply a matter of knowing what to ask for and choosing the best. They handed over credit cards and traveller's cheques for tea sets, bolts of silk material, dressing gowns, inlaid boxes, vases, bowls and bronze statuettes. By lunchtime they were worn out.

20

They went back to the hotel to eat. Light came into the high-ceilinged dining-room through blinds, shutters, curtains and screens. It was as if they were being shielded from an outside fire – having all the heat blocked out, while some of the light was admitted. About twenty other tables were occupied. Michael sat on his own, though if they had had their meal anywhere in town, he'd have eaten with them.

James looked around and smiled again. 'This ·is very pleasant,' he said. He beamed at her and added, 'I think the holiday is already doing its job. You're looking extremely well after all our shopping. Filled with a sense of achievement.'

'Yes, I'm okay now. Earlier this morning I was feeling a lot like Eadburga.'

'How's that?'

'At her worst around 8.15, or whenever it was.'

He laughed. It had taken her years to say things that made him laugh and she still didn't know what sort of remark was going to appeal to him. Sometimes he'd laugh for what seemed to be no reason at all, simply because he was in the mood.

They went up to their rooms for a rest. She closed her eyes and couldn't sleep. He got up, shuffled through the magazines and newspapers he'd already read, and said he couldn't sleep, either. They spent the afternoon making love, instead.

'Dress for dinner tonight?' she asked as she arranged her clothes in the wardrobe.

'Let's go someplace simple. I've had enough of the well-tempered cuisine. Why don't we just slouch around and walk in somewhere?'

'You wouldn't rather get the ptomaine at the end of the trip rather than straight away?'

'Well, we've got lists of doctors and hospitals a mile long. We could get a shot for it.'

'Will Michael be coming with us?'

'Of course,' he said.

'Then I guess it's safe enough.'

21

'In a pinch, I could probably protect you, too.'

'But you might get your suit creased.' She made a funny face at him.

'I love vacations,' he told her. 'You're definitely at your best.'

'I told you: I'm fine now.'

'They say most of the jet-lag hangover is caused by dehydration, but the big difference I've noticed this time is the change in light.'

'Well, it's nice to be away for a while. There'll be at least three new quarrels going by the time we get back, and they'll be missing us a lot.'

'We might take more time off sometime. A long trip. A year or so.'

'Oh, Jamie, all the sweat. I couldn't do it so soon again, setting up a whole new household and uprooting the children from all their friends.'

'I didn't mean I'd be working. I meant just you and me away from everybody in a lovely spot, somewhere like Tahiti. New Caledonia, maybe.'

She said again, 'Would Michael come too?'

'I don't know. I hadn't thought.'

She pulled a dress out by the hanger and decided that it wasn't too wrinkled to wear without having the hotel maid iron it.

'I guess he'd have to,' James said.

'He wouldn't mind?'

'Kelvin? He never minds anything. He'd love to.'

She'd have to think. If it had been Michael asking her to go away with him to the South Seas, she'd have gone like a shot. But the more dissatisfied she'd become with her life, the more reluctant she was to make any changes.

She said, 'Well, it's something to think over. When would you want to make a decision about it?'

'Three weeks, about then.'

'All right. We'll have to talk about the children. That's the main thing.'

She was still worrying about the children as they started towards the steps that led to the elevators. There was an entire puzzle-set of interlocking staircases carpeted in pale green and accompanied by carved white banisters that made the whole arrangement look like flights of ornamental balconies. If you wanted to, you could continue on down by the stairs. James always preferred to ride in elevators rather than walk. Exercise, in his opinion, was what sport was for; it wasn't meant to move you from one place to another. Locomotion should be carried out with the aid of machines and servants.

'Let me just call home again quick,' she suggested.

'You'll wake them all up. It's the wrong time there.'

'Are you sure? I'm so mixed up myself, I can't tell.'

'We'll phone when we get back from supper,' he said.

They had been on other trips together long ago, when the telephoning had become a genuine obsession. Now they had a routine for it: she mentioned it, he told her when, she believed him and agreed to abide by the times he designated. The whole game was a leftover from the unhappy years when she'd had no self-confidence and felt that she kept doing everything wrong.

Michael stepped into the elevator after them. He moved behind them as they walked through the lobby.

'Look,' Flora said.

The central fountain, which earlier in the day had been confined to three low jets, now sprayed chandelier-like cascades of brilliance into the three pools beneath. Tables and chairs had been set out around the display and five couples from the hotel were being served tea. As Flora and James watched, a group of children rushed for a table, climbed into the chairs and began to investigate the spoons and napkins. A uniformed nurse followed them.

James said, 'Like some tea?'

'Unless Michael doesn't – '

'Sure,' Michael said. 'I'll sit right over there.' He headed towards the sofas and armchairs near the reception desk. Wherever they were, he always knew where to find the best

23

spots for surveillance, and probably had a good idea where everybody else might choose to be, too. He'd been trained for all that. You couldn't see from his walk or from the way his clothes fitted that he carried guns and a knife, but he did. Sometimes it seemed incredible to Flora that he had been through scenes of violence; he'd been in the marines for two years while James was finishing up college. His placid, law-abiding face gave no sign of the fact. But she thought how upsetting the experience must have been to him at first. Even killing didn't come naturally – especially killing: somebody had to teach it to you. And boys weren't really cruel or bloodthirsty unless they had a background of brutality.

Michael's background, she knew, was quite ordinary. He was a child of an undergardener and one of the parlourmaids at the house. Once she'd asked him how he'd managed to get through his military training and he'd told her that he'd been lucky: he'd been with a group of boys who'd become really good friends. And, as for violence, he'd added, 'You got to be objective, say to yourself this is completely a professional thing. Like render unto Caesar. You know?' She had nodded and said yes, but had had no idea what he'd been talking about.

They sat close enough to the fountain to enjoy it but not so near as to be swept by the fine spray that clouded its outpourings. James had also taken care to station himself, and her, at a reasonable distance from the children, who looked like more than a match for their wardress.

Their nearest companions were a man and woman who might have been on a business trip or celebrating an early retirement. They gave the impression of being a couple who had been married for a long time. The woman looked older than the man. She had taken two extra chairs to hold her shopping bags and as soon as the tea was poured out she began to rummage through her papers and packages. She looked up and caught Flora's eye. Flora smiled. The woman said, 'I couldn't resist. It's all so pretty and the prices are just peanuts. Aren't they, Desmond?'

The man's eyes flicked to the side. 'We're going to need an extra plane to take it all back,' he said. His head turned to the stairway and the main door, warily, as if looking for eavesdroppers.

'Not here,' his wife told him.

'Only damn part of this hotel they let you smoke a pipe is in your own room. Place must be run by the anti-tobacco league.'

'Do you good,' his wife said. She began to talk about silks and jade and porcelain. Flora guessed before the woman started to quote numbers that they were going to be several price-brackets under anything she and James would have bought. On the other hand, like most rich people, she loved hunting down bargains.

The couple, whose name was Dixon, went on to tell their opinions of the city and of the country in general. They regretted, they said, not having made provision for trips outside town to – for example – the big flower festival that had been held the week before, or just the ordinary market mornings. They were leaving the next day. Flora saw James relax as he heard them say it: there wasn't going to be any danger of involvement. He began to take an interest in the list of places and shops they recommended. Flora was halfway through her second cup of tea and could tell that James would want to leave soon, when Mrs Dixon said, 'What I regret most of all, of course, is that we never got to see the goddess.'

'Oh,' Flora said. 'At the festival?'

'At her temple.'

'A statue?'

'No, no. That girl. You know – the one they train from childhood, like the Lama in Tibet.'

'Not like that,' her husband said.

'Well, I just couldn't face standing in line for all that time in the heat. But now I really wish I'd given myself more of a push.'

'I haven't heard about the goddess,' Flora admitted. James

25

said that he'd read about it somewhere, he thought, but only remembered vaguely. And he hadn't realized that the custom had to do with this part of the world.

'Oh, yes,' Mr Dixon told him, and launched into the history of the goddess, who was selected every few years from among thousands of candidates. The child was usually four or five years old when chosen, had to be beautiful, to possess several distinct aesthetic features such as the shape of the eyes and ears and the overall proportion of the limbs, and could have no blemish. 'Which is quite an unusual thing to be able to find,' he said. 'Then –'

'Then,' Mrs Dixon interrupted, 'they train her in all the religious stuff and they also teach her how to move – sort of like those temple dancers, you know: there's a special way of sitting down and getting up, and holding out your fingers, and so on. And it all means something. Something religious. There are very strict rules she's got to obey about everything – what she can eat and drink, all that. Oh, and she should never bleed. If she cuts herself – I forget whether she has to quit or not.'

'She just has to lie low for a few days, I think,' Mr Dixon said.

'And she can never cry – did I say that?'

'And never show fear.'

'Then at puberty –'

'She's out on her can and that's the whole ball game. They go and choose another one.'

'So people just drive out to her temple to look at her,' Flora asked, 'as if she's another tourist attraction?'

'Oh no, dear,' Mrs Dixon said. 'They consult her. They take their troubles to her and she gives them the solution. It's like an oracle. And I think you donate some small amount for the upkeep of the temple. They don't mind tourists, but it isn't a show – it's a real religious event.'

Mr Dixon said, 'She's very cultivated, so it seems. Speaks different languages and everything.'

James asked, 'What happens to her afterwards?'

26

'Oh, that's the joke. She used to spend the rest of her life in seclusion as the ex-goddess. But this last time, the girl took up with a young fellow, and now she's married to him and –'

'– and there's the most terrific scandal,' Mrs Dixon said happily. 'It's really turned things upside-down. I guess it's like a priest getting married to a movie star. They can't get over it.'

'Matter of fact, I wouldn't want to be in that girl's shoes.'

'Why?' Flora asked.

Mr Dixon shrugged. 'A lot of people are mad as hell. They've been led to expect one thing and now this other thing is sprung on them. They're used to thinking of their goddess as completely pure, and also truly sacred. I guess it can't look right for her to revert to being human all of a sudden, just like the rest of us. See what I mean?'

Flora nodded.

'She's broken the conventions,' James said, which didn't seem to Flora nearly such a good explanation as Mr Dixon's, but she smiled and nodded again.

* * *

They took a long time deciding where they wanted to eat their evening meal. In the beginning it was too much fun looking around to want to go inside; they had discovered the night life of the streets, full of people going about ordinary business that might have taken place indoors during the daytime: there were open-air barber shops, dress stalls where customers could choose their materials and be measured for clothes; shops that stocked real flowers and also stands that sold bouquets made out of feathers and silk.

'No wonder Mrs Dixon had all those piles of packages,' Flora said. 'Everything looks so nice.'

'Under this light,' James warned. 'I bet it's pretty tacky in daylight.'

Michael grunted his assent.

'Don't you think it's fun?' she asked.

'Very colourful,' he said. She wasn't disappointed in his answer. It gave her pleasure just to be walking beside him.

She would have liked to eat in one of the restaurants that were no more than just a few tables and chairs stuck out on the sidewalk. James vetoed the suggestion. They moved back to the beginning of richer neighbourhoods and he suddenly said, 'That one.'

In front of them was a building that looked like a joke: dragons and pagodas sprouting everywhere from its roof-tops. The lower floor was plate glass, which reassured the three of them – that looked modern and therefore unromantic and probably, they expected, hygienic. 'We can rough it for once,' James said. Through the downstairs windows they could see rows of crowded booths, people sitting and eating. Most of the patrons appeared to be tourists – another good sign.

They entered and were seated all on the same side of a table. Flora had hoped to be put between the two men, but the waiter had positioned Michael at James's far side. Opposite her an old man was eating noodles from a bowl. He stared determinedly downward.

They looked at the menu. As James ordered for them, a young couple came up and were shown to the remaining places; he had a short beard and wore a necklace consisting of a single wooden bead strung on a leather thong; she had a long pigtail down her back. They were both dressed in T-shirts and bluejeans and carried gigantic orange back-packs. They made a big production of taking off the packs and resting them against the outside of the booth. When the old man on the inside had finished eating and wanted to get out, they had to go through the whole routine again. Once they were settled, they stared across the table contemptuously at the fine clothes the others were wearing. They seemed to be especially incredulous over James's outfit, one which he himself would have considered a fairly ordinary linen casual suit for the tropics.

James switched from English to French and began to tell Flora about New Caledonia. It meant that Michael was excluded from the conversation, but he knew that this was one of James's favourite methods of detaching himself from company he didn't want to be associated with. It only worked in French because Flora's limited mastery of other languages wouldn't permit anything else. James had always been good at learning new languages. As a child he had even made up a language that he and Michael could use to baffle grown-up listeners. Occasionally they spoke it even now. Flora had figured out that it must be some variation of arpy-darpy talk, but it always went so fast that she could never catch anything.

The back-packers spoke English. He was American, she Australian. Their names were Joe and Irma. They spent their whole time at the table discussing the relative merits of two similar articles they had seen in different shops. Some part of the objects had been made out of snakeskin and, according to Irma, one of them was 'pretty ratty-looking'; on the other one, so Joe claimed, the so-called snake had been an obvious fake, definitely plastic.

'It's like those beads you got,' he said. 'Supposed to be ivory, and you can see the join where they poured it into the mould in two halves and then stuck them together. Why can't you tell? How can you miss seeing it? If you keep on spending money like this –'

Irma muttered, 'Well, it's my money.'

'We should be keeping some by for emergencies,' he said. She sulked for the rest of the meal. She chewed her food slowly and methodically. Flora wished the girl had picked everything up, thrown it all over her companion and told him to go to hell. He was staring around with disapproving interest at the other diners. He wasn't going to feel guilty about hurting his girlfriend; he hadn't even noticed her play for sympathy.

Flora said in French, 'Could you really go for a year without work?'

'Sure. I'd work on something else,' James said. 'We'd get a nice boat, sail around.' He added, 'The food isn't too bad here.'

29

'Wait till tomorrow to say it,' she told him.

* * *

The weather next morning looked like being the start of another wonderful day. All the days were wonderful in that climate at the right time of year. They both felt fine. Michael too said he was okay. Flora called home.

She got Margaret on the line, who said, 'We've missed you. Anna-Louise is on the warpath again.'

'What about?'

Anna-Louise's voice came in on an extension, saying, 'That isn't Margaret getting her story in first, is it? Flora?'

'Hi,' Flora said. 'How are you all?'

'The natives are restless, as usual.'

Margaret tried to chip in but was told by Anna-Louise to get off the line. There was a click.

'Children all right?' Flora asked.

'Couldn't be better.'

'Are they there?' She waved James over. They spent nearly fifteen minutes talking to the children, who said again how much they loved the paper doll books and how all their friends thought they were great and wanted some too. James began to look bored and to make motions that the conversation should stop. He leaned over Flora. 'We've got to hang up now,' he said into the mouthpiece.

They were the second couple into the breakfast room. 'Are we that early?' she asked.

He checked his watch. 'Only a little. It's surprising how many people use their holidays for sleeping.'

'I guess a lot of them have jet-lag, too. That's the trouble with beautiful places – they're all so far away.'

He spread out the maps as Michael was seated alone at a table for two several yards beyond them. Flora had them both in view, Michael and James. She felt her face beginning to smile. At that moment she couldn't imagine herself returning from the trip. The children and relatives could stay at the other end of the telephone.

James twitched the map into place. He liked planning things out and was good at it. She, on the other hand, couldn't even fold a map back up the right way. She was better at the shopping. Now that they were used to their routines, they had a better time sightseeing. In the early days James had spent even more time phoning his broker than Flora had in worrying about the babies.

She remembered the young couple at dinner the night before, and how much they had seemed to dislike each other. Of course, it was hard to tell anything about people who were quarrelling; still, they didn't seem to have acquired any of the manners and formulae and pleasing deceptions that helped to keep lovers friendly over long periods. She herself had come to believe that – if it weren't for this other glimpse of a love that would be for ever unfulfilled – she'd have been content with just those diplomatic gestures, plus a shared affection for what had become familiar. If she had been free to choose at this age, her life would have been different. Everybody was free now; and they all lived together before they got married.

James put a pencil mark on the map and started to draw a line across two streets.

Maybe, she thought, she'd been free even then. The freedom, or lack of it, was simply ceremonial. Rules and customs kept you from disorder and insecurity, but they also regulated your life to an extent that was sometimes intolerable. They protected and trapped at the same time. If it weren't for habit and codes of behaviour, she and Michael could have married and had a happy life together.

It had taken her years to find out that most of her troubles had been caused by trying to switch from one set of conventions to another. The people around her – even the ones who had at first seemed to be against her – had actually been all right.

She said, 'You know what I'd really like to do? I'd like to see that girl.'

'Hm?'

31

'The one the Dixons were talking about at tea. The goddess.'

'Oh.' James looked up. 'Well, maybe. But don't you think the idea is going to be a lot better than the reality? Following it up is just going to mean what they said: standing in line for hours. Do you want to spend your vacation doing that?'

'And if you don't, regretting that you never did. I would like to. Really. You don't have to come, if you don't want to.'

'Of course I'd come, if you went.'

'Could you find out about it? It's the thing I want to do most.'

'Why?'

'Why? Are there goddesses at home?'

He laughed, and said, 'Only in the museums. And in the bedroom, if you believe the nightgown ads.'

'Please.'

'Okay,' he promised. 'I'll find out about it. But it seems to me, the one worth looking at is going to be the one that went AWOL and got married.'

'She didn't go AWOL. She was retired.'

'A retired goddess? No such thing. Once a god, always a god.'

'If you become impure as soon as you bleed, then you can lose the divinity. Women – '

'All right, I'll find out about it today. Right now. This very minute.'

'I'm only trying to explain it.'

'Wasted on me,' he told her.

'Don't you think it's interesting?'

'Mm.'

'What does that mean?'

'I'll see about it this afternoon.'

Over the next few days they went to the botanical gardens; to the theatre, where they saw a long, beautiful and rather dull puppet play; and to a nightclub, at which Flora developed a headache from the smoke and James said he was pretty sure the star *chanteuse* was a man. They got dressed up in their evening clothes to visit the best restaurant in town, attended a dinner given by a friend of the family who used to be with the City Bank in the old days, and made an excursion to the boat market. Half the shops there were hardly more than floating bamboo frameworks with carpets stretched across them. Bright pink orchid-like flowers decorated all the archways and thresholds, on land and on the water. The flowers looked voluptuous but unreal, and were scentless; they added to the theatrical effect – the whole market was like a view backstage. James and Flora loved it. Michael said it was too crowded and the entire place was a fire-trap.

'Well, there's a lot of water near at hand,' James said.

'You'd never make it. One push and the whole mob's going to be everybody on top of theirselves. They'd all drown together.'

'I do love it when you get on to the subject of safety, Kelvin. It always makes me feel so privileged to be alive.'

A privilege granted to many, Flora thought, as she gazed into the throng of shoving, babbling strangers. She suddenly felt that she had to sit down.

She turned to James. 'I feel – ' she began.

He saw straight away what was wrong. He put his arm around her and started to push through the crowd. Michael took the other side. She knew that if she really collapsed, Michael could pick her up and sling her over his shoulder like a sack of flour, he was so strong. He'd had to do it once when she'd fainted at a ladies' fund-raising luncheon. That had been a hot day too, lunch with wine under a blue canvas awning outdoors; but she'd been pregnant then. There was no reason now for her to faint, except the crowd and the lack of oxygen.

There wasn't any place to sit down. She tried to slump against Michael. They moved her forward.

'Here,' James said.

She sat on something that turned out to be a tea chest. They were in another part of the main arcade, in a section that sold all kinds of boxes and trunks. A man came up to James, wanting to know if he was going to buy the chest.

Back at the hotel, they laughed about it. James had had to shell out for a sandalwood casket in order to give her time to recover. When they were alone, he asked if she was really all right, or could it be that they'd been overdoing it in the afternoons? She told him not to be silly: she was fine.

'I think maybe we should cancel the trip to the goddess, though, don't you?'

'No, James. I'm completely okay.'

'Waiting out in the sun –'

'We'll see about that when we get there,' she said flatly. It was a tone she very seldom used.

'Okay, it's your vacation. I guess we could always carry you in on a stretcher and say you were a pilgrim.'

He arranged everything for the trip to the temple. The day he chose was near the end of their stay, but not so close to the flight that they couldn't make another date if something went wrong. One of them might come down with a twenty-four-hour bug or there might be a freak rainstorm that would flood the roads. 'Or,' James said, 'if she scratches herself with a pin, we've had it till she heals up. They might even have to choose a new girl.'

In the meantime they went to look at something called 'the jade pavilion' – a room in an abandoned palace, where the silk walls had been screened by a lattice-work fence of carved jade flowers. The stone had been sheared and sliced and ground to such a fineness that in some places it appeared as thin as paper. The colours were vibrant and glowing – not with the freshness of real flowers nor the sparkle of faceted jewels, but with the lustre of fruits; the shine that came off the surfaces was almost wet-looking.

As they walked under the central trellis a woman behind them said, 'Think of having to dust this place.' A man's voice answered her, saying, 'Plenty of slave labour here. Nobody worries about dust.'

'Glorious,' James said afterwards. And Michael declared that, 'You had to hand it to them.' He'd been impressed by the amount of planning that must have gone into the work: the measuring and matching, the exactitude.

34

Flora had liked the silk walls behind, which were covered with pictures of flying birds. She said, 'I guess you're supposed to think to yourself that you're in a garden, looking out. But it's a little too ornate for me. It's like those rooms we saw in Palermo, where the whole place was gold and enamel – like being inside a jewel box. This one would have been even nicer made out of wood and then painted. Don't you think?'

'That would fade,' James said. 'You'd have to re-do it all the time. And in this climate you'd probably need to replace sections of it every few years.'

They kept calling home every day. The weather there was horrible, everyone said. Anna-Louise had a long story about friends of hers whose house had been burgled. And one of the children had a sore throat; he coughed dramatically into the receiver to show how bad it was.

'They need us,' Flora said. 'That was a cry of despair.'

'That was the standard performance,' James told her. 'There's one who hasn't inherited any bashfulness. He'd cough his heart out in front of fifty reporters every day and do retakes if he thought it hadn't been a really thorough job. No hired substitute for him. It's going to be a question of how hard we'll have to sit on him to keep him down. Worse than Teddy was at that age.'

'He sounded pretty bad.'

'You're the one we're going to worry about at the moment. One at a time. Feeling faint? Claustrophobic?'

Flora shook her head. She felt fine. They strolled around town together and sat in a public park for a while. They'd chosen a bench within the shade of a widely branched, symmetrical tree. Michael rested against the stonework of a gate some distance away. While he kept them in sight, he watched the people who passed by. James pointed out a pair of tourists coming through the entrance.

'Where?' Flora asked.

'Right by the gate. It's those two from the restaurant we went to our first night out.'

'Irma and Joe,' she said. 'So it is. And they're still arguing. Look.'

The couple had come to a stop inside the gates. Joe leaned forward and made sweeping gestures with his arms. Irma held herself in a crouching posture of defence: knees bent, shoulders hunched, chin forward. Her fists were balled up against her collar-bone. The two faced each other still encumbered by their back-packs and bearing a comical resemblance to armoured warriors or wrestlers costumed in heavy padding.

James said, 'She's just spent· all her money and he's bawling her out.'

'You give it to him, Irma,' Flora said. James squeezed her hand.

They stayed on their bench and watched a large group of uniformed schoolchildren who – under the supervision of their teachers – went through what seemed to be the usual class exercises and then began to play some game neither Flora nor James could understand. Two of the children passed a book through the group while the others counted, telling off certain players to skip in a circle around the rest. Then they all sang a rhyming verse and formed up in a new order.

At last he said, 'Okay?' and stood up. She got to her feet. In the distance Michael too stepped forward.

They were three streets from where the hired car was parked, when Flora caught sight of a yellow bowl in a store window. She slowed down and, briefly, paused to look. James and Michael moved on a few paces. She turned back, to ask James what he thought about the bowl, and a hand closed gently over her arm just above the wrist. She looked up into a face she'd never seen before. For a moment she didn't realize anything. Then the hand tightened. At the same time, someone· else grabbed her from behind. She dropped her handbag. Gasping and mewing sounds came from her throat, but she couldn't make any louder noise. She tried to kick, but that was all she could do.

Michael and James were with her almost immediately,

hitting and kicking. Michael actually threw one of the gang into the air. Flora felt herself released. She fell to her knees, with her head against the glass of the window.

'Here,' James said, 'hold on to that.' He thrust her handbag into her arms and pulled her back up. She still couldn't speak.

They hurried her to the car and drove back to the hotel. Michael came up to the room with them and sat on the edge of the bed. James said he was calling in a doctor.

'I'm all right,' she jabbered, 'all right, perfectly – I'm fine. I'm just so mad. I'm so mad I could chew bricks. The nerve of those people!' She was shaking.

Michael stood up and got her a glass of water. She drank all of it and put her head down on the bed.

'That's a good idea,' James said. He and Michael left her and went into the sitting room. She could hear them talking. Michael said, 'The cops?' and James said, 'Tied up with police on vacation. Besides, what good?'

'No hope,' Michael answered. 'Anyway, weren't after money.'

'Bag.'

'No, arm. And left it. Her, not the. Alley right next. A few more seconds.'

'Jesus Christ,' James said. 'That means.'

Michael's voice said, 'Maybe not,' and Flora began to relax. She slept for a few minutes. She was on a beach in New Caledonia and Michael was sitting beside her on the sand. There was a barrel-vaulted roof of palm leaves overhead, like the canopy of a four-poster bed. She could hear the sound of the sea. And then suddenly someone stepped up in back of her and her arms were grabbed from behind.

She woke up. She almost felt the touch still, although it had been in her dream. She stared ahead at the chairs by the bed, the green-and-yellow pattern of the material they were upholstered in, the white net curtains over the windows where the light was beginning to dim away. She thought about the real event, earlier in the afternoon, and remembered again – as if it had left a mark on her body – the moment when the hand had closed over her arm. Once more she was filled with outrage and fury. *The nerve,* she thought; *the nerve.* And the terrible feeling of having been made powerless, of being held, pinioned, captured by people who had no right to touch her. That laying of the hand on her had been like the striking of a predator, and just as impersonal. When she thought about it, it seemed to her that she was picturing all the men as much bigger and stronger than they probably were, and perhaps older, too. They might have been only teenagers.

She wanted to forget about it. It was over. And James was right: it would ruin what was left of their trip to spend it making out reports in a police station. What could the police do? These gangs of muggers hit you, disappeared around a corner and that was the end of the trail. Once in Tokyo she and James had seen a man on the opposite sidewalk robbed by two boys. His hands had suddenly gone up in the air; and there was the pistol right in broad daylight, pointing into his chest. It could happen so fast. It was the kind of street crime she had come on the holiday in order to forget.

But you had to be prepared. These things were international. And timeless. All the cruelties came back: torture, piracy, massacres. The good things didn't return so often because it took too long to develop them. And it took a whole system of convention and ritual to keep them working; wheels within wheels. She was part of it. To keep the ordered world safe, you had to budget for natural deterioration and the cost of replacement. Nothing had a very high survival rate – not even jade, hard as it was.

She thought about the pavilion of jade flowers and wondered whether it was really so beautiful. Maybe in any case it was only as good as the people who liked it believed it to be. James had loved it. Michael hadn't seemed to like it except for the evidence of the work that had been put into it. He might have disapproved of the extravagance rather than been judging the place on aesthetic grounds. She felt herself falling asleep again.

When she woke it was growing dark. She got up, took a shower and changed. The three of them ate together in the hotel dining-room, drank a great deal, had coffee and then even more to drink afterwards. They talked about law and order and decent values and Flora was tight enough to say, 'We can afford to.' They agreed not to mention the incident to anyone at home until the trip was over.

James had a hangover the next day but read through all his newspapers as usual.

'Any mention of our little drama?' she asked.

'Of course not. We didn't report it. A few other muggings here, it says.'

'Maybe they're the same ones.'

'Nope. They'd have gone for the bag and left you. These are all cases of grab-and-run.'

'You mean, they wanted to kidnap me; get you to pay ransom. So, they must know all about us, who we are, what you can raise at short notice.'

'Maybe they check up on everybody staying at big hotels. Maybe they saw your rings. Or it might just be that they know a good-looking woman when they see one: probably thought they could sell you to somebody.'

'What?'

'Sure. Hey, look what else. It says here, the ex-goddess was stoned outside her house yesterday morning.'

'Yesterday morning we were pretty stoned, too. Or was that this morning?'

'A mob threw stones at her. They were some kind of religious group.'

'That's disgusting. That's even worse than trying to kidnap people.'

'She's all right, but she's in the hospital. That ought to mean she's okay. It only takes one stone to kill somebody.'

'Disgusting,' Flora muttered.

'And interesting,' James said. 'In a lot of countries it's still the traditional punishment for adultery.'

* * *

Their hired car drove them down the coastline. They took a picnic lunch, went for a swim and visited two shrines that, according to their guidebooks, were famous. On the next day they spent the morning trying to find material for curtains to go in a house belonging to Elizabeth's mother-in-law. Michael kept close to Flora all the time; their clothes often brushed as they walked or stood side by side.

On the day of their visit to the goddess it looked for the first time during the trip as if it might rain. James went back up to their rooms and got the umbrellas. On the ride out into the country they heard a few rumblings of thunder, but after that the skies began to clear and the day turned hot and muggy. The umbrellas sat in the car while they entered the temple precincts.

They were checked at the main gate, which looked more like the entrance to a fortress than to a religious building. Flora saw James stiffen as he caught sight of the long row of invalids sitting or lying on their sides, their relatives squatting near them on the ground. She remembered his joke about pilgrims. It wasn't so funny to see the real thing. He never liked being in places where there might be diseases. Most of their travelling had been carefully packaged and sanitized to avoid coming into contact with contagion or even the grosser aspects of simple poverty. You could have all the shots you liked, and it wouldn't help against the wrong virus. She knew that he'd be telling himself again about the number and quality of the hospitals in town.

The officials looked at their papers, spoke to the driver and interpreter, and let them in. The pilgrims stayed outside on the ground. Flora wondered how long they'd have to wait, and how important it was to pay over money before you were granted an interview; or maybe the goddess did a kind of group blessing from a distance. If she wasn't even allowed to bleed, she might not be any more eager than James to get close to the diseased masses. Even when inside the courtyard you could hear a couple of them from over the wall, coughing their lungs out. The smell of decay that hung around the place might have been coming from the same source.

They were escorted across a vast, open space, through an archway, into another courtyard, across that, and to a third. The long-robed official then led them up on to the porch of one of the side buildings, around the verandah and into an assembly hall. It felt dark and cool after the walk in the open. About seventy people waited inside, some sitting on the floor and others – mainly Western tourists – either on the built-in wood bench that ran around three of the walls, or on fold-up seats they'd brought with them. There were also low stools you could borrow or rent from the temple.

The official swept forward towards a door at the far end of the hall. Two more robed figures stood on guard by it. Flora's glance flickered lightly over the other people as she passed. There weren't many children there, except for very small babies that had had to be taken along so the mother could feed them. Most of the believers or curiosity-seekers were grown up and a good proportion of them quite old. A lot of them were also talking, the deaf ones talking loudly. Perhaps the fact that one figure was on its own, not turned to anyone else, was what made Flora notice: there, sitting almost in the middle of the dark wooden floor, was Irma, resting her spine against her back-pack. Joe wasn't with her. And she looked defeated, bedraggled, lost. Maybe she'd come not because this was a tourist attraction, but because she needed advice. She still looked to Flora like the complete guru-chaser – one of those girls who went wandering around looking for some-body to tell them the meaning of life. Yet she also looked desperate in another way, which Flora thought might not have anything to do with religion or philosophy or breaking up with a boyfriend, and might simply be financial. She was so struck by the girl's attitude that she almost forgot about the goddess.

They were rushed onward. The sentries opened the double doors for them and they went through like an awaited procession, entering and leaving three more hallways, all empty and each quieter than the last, until they reached a room like a schoolroom full of benches, and were asked to sit down. Their officials stepped forward to speak with two middle-aged priestesses who had come out of the chamber beyond – perhaps the place where the goddess was actually sitting. The idea suddenly gave Flora the creeps. It was like visiting a tomb.

She whispered to James, 'Did you see Irma out there?'

'Yes.'

'I'm glad she's split up with him, but she looks terrible. I think she must be broke.'

'Probably.'

'I'd like to give her something.'

'No.'

'Not much, just – '

It would mean so little to them, Flora thought, and so much to the girl. It would be even better to be able to tell her she'd done the right thing in leaving that boy and could choose a different man now if she wanted to, and this time find one who'd really love her.

James said, 'You've got to let people lead their own lives.'

Of course, it was assuming a lot. Irma might not have broken up with Joe at all. They might be meeting again in the evening after seeing the sights separately. Even so, it was certainly true that she had run out of money. There had to be some way of helping her out, but Flora couldn't think of one. Could she just hand over some cash and say, 'Did you drop this?' Maybe she could say, 'We were in the restaurant that night and you must have left this behind, it was lying in the corner of the seat and we've been looking for you ever since.'

'She'll fall on her feet,' James told her.

'For heaven's sake. It looks like she's fallen on her head. Can't we do something?'

'I don't think so. And I don't think we should. But if you still feel the same after we get through with this, we'll see. You'll have to figure out how to work it. And don't invite her back in the car.'

Flora stared upward, thinking. She saw for the first time
that the ceiling beams were carved at regular intervals with
formal designs and they were painted in colours so bright
that they looked like enamelwork. She'd been right; that
kind of thing was much more interesting than the jade pavilion. She thought: *I'll just put some bills into an envelope and
use the story about finding it in the restaurant.* It was a shame
when people ignored their good intentions because it was
too difficult or too embarrassing to carry them out. She
usually kept a few envelopes in her pocketbook.

The interpreter came back to their bench. 'Who is the
seeker of truth?' he asked.

Flora looked blank. James said, 'What?'

'Is it you both two or three ask the goddess, or how
many?'

'Just one,' James said. 'My wife.'

The man withdrew again. He spoke to the priestesses.
One of them clapped her hands, the other went into the
next room. The robed official spoke.

'Arise, if you please,' the interpreter told them. Michael
moved from his bench to stand behind James. The three of
them stepped forward until the official put up his hand
against them.

The priestess came out again, leading a procession of
eight women like herself. They walked two by two. In the
middle of the line, after the first four and in front of the next
four they'd kept a free space, in which trotted a midget-like,
pink-clad figure: the goddess herself.

She was like a ceremonial doll only taken out on special
occasions. Her robes reached to the floor. On her head she
wore an elaborate triple-tiered crown of pearls and rubies
and some sparkling greyish glass studs that were probably
old diamonds. Long, wide earrings dangled from her ears
and continued the framing lines of the ornamentation
above, so that the still eyes seemed to float among the shim-
mering lights of crown, earrings, side panels and many-
stranded necklaces.

43

All dressed up, just like a little lady, Flora thought; *what a dreadful thing to do to that child*. And yet the face that gazed out of all its glittering trappings was not exactly that of a child: enormous, dark eyes; serenely smiling mouth; the lovely bone-structure and the refinement of the features were like those of a miniature woman, not a child. Above all, the look of utter calmness and wisdom were strange to seé. The girl could have been somewhere between seven and eight years old, although she was about the size of an American child of five.

The procession stopped. The official beckoned to Flora. She came up to where he pointed. The child, who hadn't looked at anything particular in the room, turned to her with pleased recognition, like a mother greeting a daughter.

Flora bowed and smiled back, slightly flustered but tingling with gratification. *This is weird*, she thought. *This is ridiculous*. But as the procession wheeled around, heading back into the room it had come from and gathering her along with it, she knew she would follow wherever they went and for however long they wanted her to keep going. She was actually close to tears.

The room was not a room, only another corridor. They had to walk down several turnings until they emerged at a courtyard of fruit trees. They entered the audience chamber from the far side.

The goddess seated herself on a wooden throne raised on steps. Like the rafters in this room too, the throne was carved and painted. She sat on a cushion of some ordinary material like burlap, which made her robes appear even more luxurious by contrast. Her tiny feet in their embroidered magenta slippers rested on one of the steps.

A robed woman, who had been waiting for them in the room, came and stood behind and a little to the side of the throne like a governess or a chaperone. Flora wondered if in fact the woman was to be the one to hand out the answers.

The little girl smiled prettily and said, 'Please sit.' She indicated the hassock in front of the steps to the throne. Flora knelt. She was uncomfortable. Her skirt felt too tight and her heart was thumping heavily. She raised her glance to the child and met, from out of all the silks and jewels, a look of happy repose.

'Speak freely,' the child told her in a musical voice. 'And say what is in your heart.'

Flora swallowed. She could hear the loud sound it made in her throat. All at once tears were in her eyes. She saw the figure before her in a blur, as if it might have been a holy statue and not a human being.

She began, 'I don't know what to do. Year after year. My life is useless. I have everything, nothing to want. Kind husband, wonderful children. I feel ashamed to be ungrateful, but it never was what . . . it never seemed like mine. It's as if I'd never had my own self. But there's one thing: a man. He's the only one who isn't corrupted, the only one I can rely on. I think about him all the time. I can't stop. I can't stand the idea that we'll never be together. He's only a servant. And I don't know what to do. I love him so much.' She ended on a sob and was silent.

She waited. Nothing happened. She sniffed, wiped the back of her hand across her cheek and looked up for her answer.

'Love?' the goddess asked.

Flora nodded. 'Yes,' she mumbled. 'Yes, yes.'

'True love', the sweet voice told her, 'is poor.'

Poor? Flora was bewildered. *Pure*, she thought. *Of course.*

'It is from the sky.'

The chaperone leaned forward towards the jewelled head. 'Godly,' she hissed.

'Godly?' the child repeated, smiling into Flora's anxious face. The densely embellished right sleeve raised itself as the girl lifted her arm. The small hand made a lyrical gesture up towards the heavens and back in an arc to the ground: a movement that described beauty and love falling upon human lovers below, uniting as it touched them – bringing together, inevitably, her life and Michael's without greed or insistence.

45

'Yes, yes,' she stammered again. She felt stunned. She knew that she had had her answer, whatever it was. It would take her some time to figure out exactly what it meant.

The child hadn't finished. 'You must rise above,' she said thoughtfully. 'You must ascend.'

'Transcend,' the chaperone corrected.

'Ascend,' the child repeated.

Flora nodded. She sighed and said, 'Thank you.' She started to get up. The chaperone came forward and, without touching, showed her the directions in which she should go. For a moment the woman blocked any further sight of the child. She indicated that Flora should move away, not try to catch another glimpse of the goddess, not to say thank you again; the interview was over.

She walked clumsily from the chamber and staggered a few times as she followed two priestesses back to the waiting-room. She bowed farewell to everyone. She let James take her by the arm. As they were ushered out, she leaned against him.

As soon as they passed outside the main gates, he began to hurry her along.

'Why are we going so fast?' she complained.

'Because you look terrible. I want to get you back into the car. You look like you're ready to faint again.'

'You're going too fast. I can't keep up.'

'Try, Flora,' he said. 'We can carry you if we have to.'

'No.'

'Christ knows why I let you talk me into this. What did she do – say she saw the ace of spades in your palm, or something? Jesus.' He and Michael bundled her into the car and they started on the drive to town.

She fell back in the seat. She still couldn't think clearly. *I must ascend*, she thought. It might be painful, but it would be necessary. *Did she mean that I have to rise above earthly love?* Maybe what the goddess had meant was that in the end everyone died and went to heaven, so it wasn't worth getting upset over unimportant things.

46

And perhaps the girl had also meant exactly what she'd said about love – that it was from heaven, freely given and necessary, but that rich people never had to feel necessity; if a friendship broke down, or a marriage, or a blood relationship, they somehow always managed to buy another one. Life could be made very agreeable that way. But love was what the goddess had said it was – not pure: poor.

'Well?' James asked.

'Better,' she said.

'Thank God for that. What did the creature do to you?'

'She told me I had to rise above.'

'Rise above what?'

'Oh, everything, I guess.'

'And that's what knocked you out – the Eastern version of moral uplift?'

'I just suddenly felt sort of . . . I don't know.'

He bent towards her, kissed her near her ear and whispered, 'Pregnant.'

'No.'

'Sure? You've been close to fainting twice.'

'Yes,' she said. 'Yes, I'm sure. No. What did you think of it all, Michael?'

'Very interesting indeed,' Michael answered. 'It's another way of life.'

'What did you think of her? The goddess.'

'Cute-looking little kid, but skinny as a rail underneath all those party clothes. You wonder if they feed them enough.'

'Those hundreds of people on litters believe she can cure them.'

'Yeah, well, they're sick. Sick people believe in anything.'

'Maybe they're right. Sometimes if you have faith, it makes things true.'

James groaned slightly with impatience.

Michael said, 'It's deception. Self-deception always makes people feel good. But it wouldn't fix a broken leg, if that's what was wrong with you. It might help you get better quicker, once a doctor's done the real work – see what I mean?'

'Yes, I see,' she said. He didn't understand. But there was no reason why he should. James said that she was tired and upset. 'We'll be back soon,' he assured her. 'And let's have an early lunch. I'm hungry as hell from getting up so early.'

'Is it still morning? You didn't think much of her, either, did you?'

'I thought she looked great, really fabulous – the dress, like a walking cyclamen plant, and the whole effect very pretty but a bit bizarre: like a gnome out of a fairy-tale. What I don't like is how she's knocked the wind out of you. They aren't supposed to do that. They're supposed to give comfort and strength. That's the nature of the job.'

'She did. She gave me something to think about, anyway. All the rest was me trying to get out what I wanted to say.'

He held her hand. He didn't ask what her request had been. He probably thought he knew; he'd think she'd have wanted to know something like, 'Why can't I be happy?' Everybody wanted happiness.

The car speeded up along the stretches by the coastline. They opened the windows and got a whiff of the sea before returning to the air-conditioning. Flora breathed deeply. All beaches were the same: salt and iodine, like the summers of her childhood. New Caledonia would be like this, too.

They reached town before noon. James ordered the car to wait down a side street. The three of them got out and walked to one of the nice restaurants they had tried several times before. Flora was all right now, except that she felt bemused. She could walk without any trouble but she couldn't stop thinking about the temple and the goddess. She especially couldn't stop remembering the expression of joyful serenity on the child's face. It seemed to her that if she kept up the attempt to recapture the way it looked, she wouldn't have to let go of it.

The whole business had gone very quickly, as matters usually did when well-organized, and paid for, in advance. And now they were having a good meal in a comfortable restaurant; and only at that moment did Flora recall that

48

she'd meant to go up to Irma on her way out and hand her some money in an envelope.

'Eat,' James said.

She shook her head.

'Just a little,' he insisted.

She picked up the china spoon and looked at it. She put it into the soup bowl. James watched patiently. When the children had been small, he was always the one who could make them eat when they didn't want to, and later, make them brush their teeth: he let you know, without saying anything, that he was prepared to wait for ever, unchanging and with arms folded, until you did the right thing. Authority. And he never bothered with modern ideas about explaining things rationally. If the children asked, 'Why do I have to?' he'd answer, 'Because I say so.'

She began slowly, then ate hungrily. Before the coffee, she went off to the ladies' room for a long time and while she was there made sure that her face and hair looked perfect. She even thought of brushing her teeth with the travelling toothbrush she carried in her purse, but she'd be back at the hotel soon – she could do it there. James smiled approvingly as she emerged.

They sauntered out into the hot, dusty street again.

'Museum?' he suggested, 'or siesta?'

'A little nap might be nice. Is that all right with you, Michael?'

'Sure, fine,' Michael said.

James stopped on the corner. 'Where was that museum, anyhow?' he asked. 'Down around that street there somewhere, isn't it?'

Michael looked up. He began to point things out in the distance. Flora kept walking around the bend as the street curved to the right. She drew back against the buildings to avoid three boys who were standing together and talking in whispers. But as soon as she was clear, two others came out of a doorway. She started to move away, but they came straight towards her. And suddenly the first three, their

49

friends, were behind her, snatching at her arms. It was the same as the day before, but this time she screamed loudly for Michael before the hands started to grip over her eyes and mouth. She also kicked and thrashed while they dragged her along the sidewalk. Right at the beginning, except for her own outburst, all the violent pulling and shoving took place to the accompaniment of low mutters and hisses. Only when James and Michael came charging around the corner did the real noise begin.

The gang had guns. The man now left alone to hold Flora from behind was jabbing something into her backbone. She knew it was a gun because she saw two of the others pull out pistols. They went for James. The voice behind her yelled, 'Stop, or we kill the woman.' Flora kept still, in case her struggling caused the weapon to go off by mistake. But Michael had his own gun in his hand and was crouched down in the road. He shot the two who were heading towards James, the third, who was waving a pistol in the air, and there was a fourth explosion landing someplace where Flora couldn't see. The arm around her gripped so tightly that she was suffocating. The voice, sounding deranged, screamed into her ear, 'You drop the gun, or I kill her!' She knew he meant it. He'd do anything. He might even kill her without knowing what he was doing.

Michael didn't hesitate. She saw him turn towards them and the look on his face was nothing: it was like being confronted by a machine. He fired right at her. She should have known.

She didn't fall straight away. The man who had held her lay dead on the ground while she swayed above him. She knew she'd been shot, but not where. It felt as if she'd been hit by a truck. And suddenly she saw that there was blood everywhere – maybe hers, maybe other people's.

She should have known that a man formed by the conventions of the world into which she had married would already have his loyalties arranged in order of importance, and that the men and male heirs to the line would always

50

take precedence over the outsiders who had fitted themselves into their lives. James was central; she was only decoration. As long as one man in the street was left with a gun, that was a danger to James. In Michael's eyes she had passed during less than three minutes from object to obstacle. He'd shot her to pieces, and, using her as a target, killed the gunman behind her.

James had his arms around her. He was calling out for an ambulance. There were plenty of other people on the street now. And she thought: *My God, how embarrassing: I've wet my pants.* But what she said was, 'I'm bleeding,' and passed out.

* * *

She woke up looking at a wall, at window-blinds, at the ceiling. Everything hurt.

It was still daylight, so perhaps she hadn't been there very long. Or maybe it was the next day. It felt like a long time. She was trussed like a swaddled baby and she was hooked up to a lot of tubes – she could see that, too. And she was terrified that parts of her body had been shattered beyond repair: that they would be crippled so badly that they'd never move again, that perhaps the doctors had amputated limbs. The fear was even worse than the pain.

Someone got up from behind all the machinery on her other side and left the room.

James came from around the back of her bed and sat in a chair next to her. He looked tired. And sad, too. That was unusual; she'd hardly ever seen him looking sad. He reached over and put his hand on her bare right arm, which lay outside the covers. She realized that she must be naked underneath; only bandages, no nightgown.

'You're going to be all right,' he told her.

She believed him. She said, 'Hurts a lot.' He smiled grimly. She asked, 'How long have I been here?'

'Twenty-four hours.'

'You haven't shaved.'

51

He kept squeezing her arm lightly and looking into her face. She thought she was about to go back to sleep again, but he caught her attention by saying her name.

'Would you do something for me?'

She said, 'Of course. You're always so good to me.'

He put his head down on the bed for a while and sighed. He really did love her, she thought, but she'd never believed it before.

'If you could talk to Michael,' he said. 'Just a couple of seconds. He feels so broken up about how it happened. If you could just let him know you understand.'

'I understand,' she said.

'I mean, tell him you forgive him. He hasn't said much, but he hasn't been able to eat or sleep, either. Or shave. Can I tell him to come in?'

She suddenly sensed that everything was draining away from her, never to return. She tried to hold on, but it was no use.

'Flora?'

The horror passed. She felt better. The fear had left, along with all the rest. She knew that she was going to die.

'Yes,' she said. 'Tell him to come in.'

James went away. She heard his footsteps. And Michael's; heard James saying, 'Just a couple of seconds. She's very tired,' and saw him moving away out of the room as Michael sat down in the chair. She turned her head to look at him.

He was smiling. Even with her head to the side, she could see his expression exactly: a nasty little smile. His drunken uncle had been chauffeur and pander to the old man and his cousins; and, of course, Michael would have taken over the same office for the sons. She should have known. It was that kind of family: even the employees were inheritable.

Everything was obvious now, and especially the fact that Michael's unshakeable politeness and deference had been an indication of his distaste for her. He'd given up pretending, now that he knew she was dying. It was more than distaste. It must be a real hatred, because he couldn't help it any longer. He wanted to show her, even with James just outside the door.

'I want you to understand,' he said quietly.

'No need,' she answered.

'You got to understand, it's for him. Far as I'm concerned, I don't give a shit. You've just got to tell him you forgive me. Then it'll be okay.'

Everything would be all right. It was simple, if you had that much money. When they reported the attack, James would see to it that everyone thought she'd been shot by the kidnappers, not by Michael. Who would question it? Two respectable witnesses; and dead men who were known criminals. The hospital would get a new wing, the police force a large donation. It would be easy. It would have been easy even if they'd deliberately set out to murder her and hired the men to do it.

'If it was me,' Michael said, leaning forward, 'I'd be counting the minutes till you go down the tubes. "Oh James dear, look at that, oh isn't that perfectly sweet? Can I have the car window open, if it's all right with Michael: can I have it closed, if Michael doesn't mind?" Pain in the ass is what you are. I mean, I seen plenty: one to a hundred I used to mark them, and you rate down around ten, sweetheart. A real lemon. "Am I doing this right, am I doing that?" I told him, "Jimbo, this one's a dud." And he just said, "No, Kelvin, this time I'm choosing for myself." He wouldn't listen.'

James could do it right next time, she thought. He'd marry again, perhaps quite soon, and be just as content. He'd probably go to New Caledonia after all, maybe with another woman, or just with Michael. Someone else would bring up her children, no doubt doing it very well. They'd have the photographs of her, so everyone could remember how pretty she'd been; she had always taken a good picture. The family would be able to choose the new wife, as they'd chosen for Edward. She'd been crazy about Edward; that was how everything had started. It was enough to make you laugh. But she had to stop thinking about it. She had to ascend. All the events in the house and all the holiday travelling would still go on, only she wouldn't be able to have any part in them. She had to rise above.

'I forgive,' she said. It was becoming difficult for her to speak.

'I'll get him,' Michael told her. He stood up.

'Wait.' She started to breathe quickly.

He leaned across the bed to look at her face. He said, 'I'll get somebody.'

'Michael,' she said clearly, 'I loved you.'

He stepped back. The smile vanished. He looked revolted, infuriated.

'I loved you,' she repeated. 'With all my heart.' Her lips curved together, her eyes closed, her head moved to the side. She was gone.

Michael began to scream.

The sound brought James running into the room, and two nurses after him.

Michael caught Flora up in his arms. He shouted into her closed face. He tried to slam her against the wall. James pulled him back. 'It's all right,' he said. 'Stop.'

'Bitch,' Michael yelled at Flora. 'Take it back. Take it back, you lousy bitch.'

'Calm down,' James said. 'She forgives you.' He got his arm around both of them and tugged. Michael let go, dropping Flora's body. She fell face downward. The nurses stooped to pick her up from the floor.

James and Michael stood grappled together, their faces wet with tears and sweat. Michael stared at the wall in front of him.

'It's all right,' James told him. 'She understands. Don't worry. After people die, they understand everything.'

ON ICE

Beverley moved to Munich during the late summer. She found a room with a German family, enrolled as an auditor at the university and got to know her way around the town. In the evenings she went out with her German boyfriend, Claus.

They had met the year before, on the boat coming over; they'd all – her parents, too – been travelling on a charter deal that had worked out cheaper than most air fares at the time. Claus had been going out with an older girl in the big crowd she'd been with, but he'd given her his address. And so when the family was back in America, she'd looked him up.

In the spring he'd asked her to marry him. She'd said yes. From the moment of meeting him she hadn't considered anything else: that he could leave her, or that one of them might die, or that he might have been the kind of man to seduce girls and leave them flat or to carry on two affairs at the same time. She hadn't really considered much at all. She'd simply thought she'd stop living if she couldn't be with him.

He was ten years older, already a settled man: a doctor. Because of his work she didn't see as much of him as she'd have liked to; sometimes he couldn't tell when he'd be on duty. He'd show up late. In fact, he was hardly ever on time for anything. She accepted the fact that it was the job that was to blame. Since she loved him, she didn't question it. Once he turned up two days later than he'd said he would.

Now they were together nearly all the time. They had separate addresses and they ate their meals out, but she was pretty sure that in another two months or so they'd announce their engagement officially and maybe get married in the spring, or at the beginning of the summer. She wanted to go to college, but that too would work out somehow.

He had taken his holiday so that they could spend Christmas and New Year's together. He'd booked the rooms and everything. She bought a parka and a pair of ski pants and was looking forward to the trip. She'd never been on skis.

The night before he was to pick her up, she packed her suitcase, turned out the lights in her room and took a last look across the street at the steep roofs and studio apartments opposite. A thin layer of snow lay in patterns over every ridge and line. The light was off in the glass-roofed atelier where a dark-haired young man – probably a painter or sculptor – lived on his own. She used to see him from time to time when she passed by the window, or stood there to open the inner panes and put her milk and butter next to the outer ones to keep cold. One day he had waved frantically at her. And, instinctively, she had ducked away out of sight. Afterwards she'd been furious with herself, and wanted to see him again so she could wave back, as she should have done in the first place. But he was never there. It upset her that she might have hurt his feelings – that she'd been so prim and suspicious. That was the way she was, unluckily, because that was the way her family liked people to be, especially women. That was the way she was with everyone but Claus.

He arrived early, for once. His skis were strapped to the top of the car; she'd have to hire a pair when they got to the village. The weather was good for driving and Claus was in a lighthearted mood. They kissed as the car went up and down the hills, around the corners. They couldn't wait till Christmas to give each other their presents, so they stopped and opened them in the car. They'd each chosen the same thing – a scarf. But he so clearly preferred the one he'd bought for her, even telling her he didn't think much of the other's colour scheme, that she said, 'Well, they're both the same size. We can switch.' She took off the one he'd given her and handed it to him. It was a gesture of anger. She didn't imagine he'd want to take her up on the offer.

'I suppose we might as well,' he said. He held up his scarf
and smiled at it. Beverley too liked her own choice better, but
she would never have said so. She would never have been so
brutal to someone she was fond of. On the other hand, she
realized that he didn't often dare to be honest with anyone. It
was like her reaction to the painter living across from her: not
being able to wave back.

They drove right over the top of the big mountain passes
and pulled up near a lookout station where three tourist
buses were parked. Some of the sightseers were out explor-
ing the gravelly surface of the glacier formations left over
from the Ice Age, some were gathered around the hut that
sold soft drinks and sandwiches. Claus and Beverley got out
and walked to the grey mass of gritty material on the far side
of the road. The air seemed to be colder when they reached it,
the sun to go in. It wasn't at all the way a glacier out of the
past should look. It was curved like the back of a turtle; dull,
dirty and – as Beverley said – reminiscent of ordinary con-
crete. She was disappointed. She liked old things to have an
air of splendour and romance.

Claus, in contrast, was mildly interested. Facts appealed to
him. He didn't care so much about looks, although he was
always telling her that something she'd be wearing wasn't
straight, and he'd often put out a hand to neaten her hair. He
was shocked that she could get along with a safety pin
instead of taking the trouble to sew back a button that had
come off. She could go for weeks without mending something torn.

He couldn't understand such habits and behaviour. The
slovenliness of it all horrified him. But she knew that her
carelessness was one of the things about her that most
attracted him. Secretly he would have liked to be more
bohemian, to live in the artists' quarter, never to have to say
yes–sir–no–sir to the top surgeons who came around on
inspection in the mornings wearing white gloves, who shook
hands with everyone from top to bottom of the building and
then, according to popular belief, peeled off the gloves,

57

flinging them away for the assistant to pick up and take to the
laundry or, perhaps, destroy. She was sure he had dreams of
tearing all his buttons off and going to work covered in safety
pins. He hated his own respectability while prizing the public
and cultural disciplines that forced people into repression. He
was civilized and he was frustrated. Beverley cured the
frustration while he was curing other people's illnesses.

On the other side of the pass they followed the route of the
mountain stream – a swift, icy green torrent that raced along
beside them. 'This is more like it,' she said.

The village they were in was down in the valley. Up on the
peaks were several larger, more fashionable and more
expensive winter resorts, including the famous Hotel Miramar, whose rooms were said to be like art galleries for the *art
nouveau* period.

Their hotel was small and overcrowded. Their room was
actually not in the main building at all but in what was
obviously a private house let out to accommodate tourists
and make the owners some money during the season. There
were many places in the world where a family could live for
the rest of the year on what the house brought in during a
few weeks of skiing, or sailing, or whatever was the main
attraction of the region. A lot of the Cape was like that, back
home.

The hotel dining-room was in the main building and had
space enough for twenty tables, some seating four people.
Theirs was just for two. The food was good – a combination
of German and Italian cooking, and there was a lot to eat. The
crisp, clear air and the exercise made Beverley hungry all day
long.

Claus took her out on a slope where they could be alone
and taught her how to ski downhill. It was much easier than
being on the T-bar lifts, but even so, she spent most of her
time picking herself up. He hadn't taught her how to turn a
corner. When she began to go so fast that she was about to
crash, she'd fall down deliberately, to save herself, and then
get up and start over again. She wished that she had short

skis like the ones they gave children to practise on. All the children she saw could ski better than she could.

They spent Christmas Eve in the hotel. The proprietor, a wolfish-looking man with suave manners, smiled aimiably at them. He leaned over their chairs to talk to them about the weather and the state of the snow. His name was Lucas, but when speaking of him between themselves, they referred to him as Lupus, because of the way he looked.

There were three other couples in the dining-room. Christmas was a time for the family. Those who had chosen to leave their relatives went out to the bars and dance-floors in search of crowds to replace them. Beverley started to drink more and more, to think about her parents opening their presents. She also wondered how much Claus loved her and whether she was always going to be able to get along with him, not to mention his family. She'd met his mother once and couldn't stand her. But that didn't matter; she loved him. She'd never love anyone else. Tears came into her eyes.

'What are you thinking?' he asked.

'About our Christmas scarves. It isn't right.'

'I thought you didn't like mine.'

'You were the one. You didn't like mine. I'm sorry. I thought it was so nice. And I actually do like it better. But I want the one you chose for me. Don't you understand?'

He said yes, he did. And they gave back their scarves on the way out, so that instead of having what they liked and being unhappy about it, they were happy despite not liking what they had.

After Christmas the whole village filled up fast. They'd been lucky to get in quickly and rent the skis. Every pair in the place had now been claimed by someone. There were people standing in line and looking at their watches for skis to become free. The night-life too speeded up. The frozen alleyways were full of partygoers on their way to and from the taverns. There was singing in the evenings; you could hear voices calling across the snow, laughter from all the doorways as people burst from lighted interiors into the cold

59

night air and the whiteness of the snow that retained its shine
even in the dark.

The best hotel down in the village was the Adler. It also
had a good restaurant, very large, and a beer cellar. A painted
wooden eagle hung over the doorway and everything inside
was cheerful and spotless. You could tell it was the kind of
place that would have geraniums in windowboxes when the
weather turned warmer. They went there twice for dinner.
On the second evening, just as they were leaving, a voice
called out in English, 'Bev – hey, Bev-er-ley!'

She turned around. She didn't know for a moment which face
to look at. Someone was waving at her. She stepped forward.
And there was Angela, a friend from school, with five other
American college kids all her age. It was unexpected; until that
moment it had been unthinkable to Beverley that both her lives,
one on either side of the Atlantic, should suddenly join up. She
felt strongly that although she had always liked her fairly well,
Angela should really have stayed in America.

'Hi, Beverley.'

'Hi, Ange. What a surprise.'

Angela quickly introduced the other friends: Darell, Tom,
Mimi, Liza and Rick.

Beverley had to introduce Claus.

'Sit down,' Angela said. 'Join us for a beer.' She looked at
Claus invitingly. Beverley spoke to him in German, saying
that they had to meet friends: didn't he remember?

'Gee,' Angela said, 'you sure can rattle it off, can't you?'

'Sort of,' she said. If you couldn't speak another language
after a year in bed with a foreigner, you might as well give
up. 'Where are you staying?' she asked.

'Here.'

'For how long?'

'Another week.'

'I'll be in touch,' Beverley said. 'Tonight I'm afraid we've
got to meet some people.' She headed towards the door
again. Claus followed. When they were outside, he asked her
why she hadn't wanted to stay.

She tried to explain: about the way it was back home, the gossip, everything. To run around on European vacations with your friends and probably – like rich Angela – be fooling around with all of them, was one thing; but to be falsely registered in a hotel as the wife of a foreign man ten years older than you were, was another. Nobody at home would understand. It wasn't the way people behaved there.

'I bet it is,' he said. 'I bet they do it all the time, like everywhere else.'

'But certain things are illegal. In the state I come from it's even illegal to buy a contraceptive if it's for preventing pregnancy. You can only get them on the excuse that they're to prevent venereal disease. It's all to do with religion. It's supposed to be a country with a secular government, but all the laws about sex assume it's something bad. Unless it really is bad; if it's rape, you need two independent witnesses to prove it. I just don't know that I want to spend all our holiday drinking beer with those people, do you?'

'Of course not,' he said. 'Why are you so upset?'

She put her arm around him and said she wasn't upset. But he was right, she realized. She hated it that the others had discovered her secret, happy life.

* * *

The next day, after lunch, he told her that he wanted to try one of the high slopes and get a good run down the mountainside.

'I asked Lupus about the timing, but it depends on the snow. I may be a little late. You could go see your friends at the Adler, if you like.'

'I'll wait at the room for you,' she said.

It was nearly dark when he came in. He was laughing. He stripped off his clothes, wrapped himself in a towel and went across the hall to the bathroom, where they had an enormous tub as big as a bed.

He'd fallen several times. She gathered that it had actually been very dangerous, and there wouldn't have been anybody else around if he'd been seriously injured.

'Look,' he said, picking his ski pants up off the chair. 'They're all ripped. That's my only pair, too. I'll have to ski in my suit.'

'I'll sew them,' she offered. She got out the pocket sewing kit she'd bought because it looked pretty. The only things in it she'd ever used were the safety pins, although everything was there: needles, thread, a few buttons and a thimble. She sat on the chair and sewed up the long tear in the material while he changed his clothes.

'It isn't very straight,' she said. The stitches were large, the sewing like that of a child. The mend resembled a badly healed wound. But Claus was delighted. 'As long as it holds together,' he told her, and she felt proud of herself.

At supper he said he thought that the next day he'd try the neighbouring run.

'Are you sure it's okay?' she asked. 'If it's so risky, and there isn't anybody else around? You could break a leg.'

'Doctors don't break things. It's like lawyers – they never go to law.'

'Lawyers can choose. They don't do it, because they know what it costs. Anybody can break a leg.'

'Will you mind being alone down here?'

'No, that's all right.'

'You could go up the mountain to the other hotels.'

'I could even go to the really fancy place, couldn't I? They probably don't let anyone in that isn't a guest.'

'They'd let you into everything except the hotel, I think. That's a good idea. I wouldn't mind going up there, too. You can tell me what it's like. I just want to get some real exercise first. You never know what the weather might do.'

She said all right: she'd go up to the big hotel the next day.

*   *   *

A man who worked one of the ski lifts pointed out the right road to her. She was glad of her good German, which was perfectly understood even where the populace spoke more Italian and had grown up with a local language that hadn't mixed with other European tongues since shortly after Roman times. She had heard fellow Americans asking directions in English and having a spate of the home-grown dialect loosed off at them.

She bought a chocolate bar to eat later, instead of lunch, with a cup of coffee. She'd become almost addicted to a particular kind of milk chocolate that had pieces of nougat baked into it. The bar was triangle-shaped and each wedge a triangle when broken off.

She had a quiet ride up. The cable car was large, painted a dark green. There were three other people travelling with her – a young boy who carried a pair of skates, and an old couple, very well-dressed. The woman was carefully made-up, her fur coat looked soft and bushy, her fur-trimmed boots were the kind you wore for sitting down on the observation platform rather than trudging through the snow. Her husband's coat had an astrakhan collar that matched the hat he wore. The cane he held between his knees was topped by a silver knob worked to resemble a piece of wood with knots in it. Both man and woman looked as if they belonged up at the top of the mountain, at the luxury hotel: Beverley wondered why they had gone down to the valley at all. They began to speak quickly in a language she couldn't place.

She looked out of the windows at the blazing white plains and fields, the long swoop of drifts that ran from the crests to a point where the line of the mountainside shot out into infinity. The boy started to whistle and kicked the wall near his seat.

When they arrived at the top, there was a delay. They hung where they had stopped, the doors remaining shut. The old couple stood up to look. Beverley and the boy were already on their feet.

They could see two stretchers being carried by, the bodies each covered with a white sheet and red blanket; then a third, and the person being carried was fighting to throw the covers off. As the stretcher-bearers hurried past, a hand flung away the blanket and Beverley caught a glimpse of a head entirely red, the crown looking as if it had been cut by an axe, and the mouth open but not producing a sound. She shut her eyes and put her head down. She could hear the old couple murmuring to each other in their own language; they sounded strangely casual, as if the vision hadn't caused them much concern. Perhaps they hadn't seen so much; perhaps their eyesight wasn't very good any more.

When the doors finally opened, she'd forgotten about coffee and the hotel and everything. She thought she'd like to sit down and drink a beer and try to wipe away the memory of the man who'd been hurt. It might even have been a woman – you couldn't tell much from a head and face so badly injured. But she had a feeling it had been a man. And she was sure that he wasn't going to live.

She began to plod along the snow-packed lanes to the centre of the village. Just as she was thinking of going into one of the taverns ahead, she came in view of the Hotel Miramar above and beyond her, shining like a castle at the top of the hill. She stood admiring it for a few seconds, then turned into a side street.

She almost skidded on a patch of ice around the corner. Opposite her was a restaurant. She went in and sat down. The waiter was an old man with white hair and a white moustache. He didn't think it unusual that she should order just a beer, alone, in the middle of the morning. A group of men in suits were seated around a table at the back; the place was obviously for locals, not for the foreign skiers. When the waiter brought the beer, she said, 'As I came up, in the cable car, I saw a man. Has there been an accident? They were carrying people. Blood.'

'Ah, the ice wall,' he said. 'We warn everybody, but they still have to try it, to prove how good they are.'

'What is it?'

'It's a wall of ice in the middle of the toboggan run. If you haven't been braking and using your skill to turn at the corners, you go over the bank and into the wall. It's solid ice.'

'They were bleeding all over.'

'Ice is very hard. Hard as stone. Hard as steel. The speeds you can achieve going downhill – fantastic.'

'Does it happen a lot?'

'Quite often, yes. We try to discourage people from going, but you can't.'

She began to drink her beer. He told her that there was another attraction, an ice maze, which was also popular but considerably less dangerous, as the walls were only about a metre high and the gradient not too steep; people used special puffy cushions to slide through it. Children loved it. It was one of the Miramar entertainments that was open to the public.

She asked directions to the ice maze and the skating rink. When she was ready to leave, he came outside the door with her and pointed up the hillside.

It was a long way up. She was out of breath by the time she started to climb the steps. And they were slippery, too. The handrail was coated with ice. She wondered what everything would look like in the summer, how different it would be. There were lakes in the neighbouring valleys; people would probably be lolling around in deck-chairs and trying to pick up a suntan. And the famous skating rink, she suddenly remembered, could be turned into a swimming pool. If Claus ever wanted to come back to the place in warmer weather, she'd be able to join him then up on the mountainside – not that she was an expert at hiking or rock-climbing either, but at least she could go for a long walk. Not knowing how to ski meant that their time was going to be divided. She hadn't thought about that before they'd arrived.

She bought a visitor's ticket and stood by the side of the rink until she felt cold. She was too self-conscious to put on a pair of skates herself. It was all right to watch, but to get out and slide around all on your own would be futile. She couldn't see anyone who was without a friend or relative. Claus was out on the slopes alone, but skiing was different. And he was a man; that made a difference, too.

She managed to find a perfect place in the after-ski lounge, a small table next to the vast plate-glass window that overlooked the rink. She brought two cups of coffee to it, drank one, started on the first section of her chocolate bar and was about to break off another piece when she heard a voice saying, 'Well, here you are again.'

It was Angela. She sat down in the second chair. She was wearing a top-to-toe outfit made of some silvery, shiny material that looked as if it might have been designed for an astronaut. She pushed her dark glasses to the top of her head, undid the earphones of her Walkman and said it was great running into each other again.

Civilization, Beverley thought, was what stopped people from telling someone like Angela to shove her earphones up her nose and get lost. 'Been skiing?' she asked.

'Till I fell on my duff,' Angela said.

'Alone?'

'No, the whole gang's here. What about you? Got your Mr Gorgeous with you? Who is he?'

'A friend,' she said.

'Some friend. He looks – you know. All those cheekbones and everything. Really European.'

'He is European.'

'I mean, like he looks. He looks European. You know?'

'Sure,' Beverley said. 'Who-all are you with?'

'Oh, just that bunch you saw the other night.'

'Who are they?'

'Well, Liza went to school with me those last two years. Tom and Rick are in my class: economics and government studies. Then, Mimi and Darell – how can I describe them?'

'Lovers?'

'No, silly.' She gave Beverley's arm a coy little push. 'Mimi and Darell are sort of in the group, except they actually didn't quite make it. First of all they were too late, and then she started to have all these doubts. So they aren't officially registered with the organization.'

'What organization?'

66

'The Fountain of Light.'

'The what?'

'It's our Christian fellowship foundation. We bring the culture and hope of the free world to – '

Beverley removed the saucer covering her second cup of coffee.

Angela's expression became fixed and devout. She gabbled about 'the word', the need for real estate, 'the light' and the building of training centres; 'the fountain'; the establishing of weekly lectures in notable beauty spots, the investment of cash in long-term plans for truth, light, love and a whole lot else, including medical research. Very few people outside the movement knew, she said, that vitamin intake was directly related to disorders of the personality. But some day there would be 'detoxification clinics' all over the world, where people could go to profit from the word.

'To read?'

'To resolve their vitamin imbalance, Bev. To reach God. We'd like to start up an education programme right here.'

Beverley stopped listening and drank. For Angela to have turned out to be a run-of-the-mill brainless co-ed was bad enough. For her to be part of a maverick cult bringing fountains of light anywhere was worse, though possibly slightly more interesting. She said, 'I don't know how much luck you'll have trying to give away culture and hope around here. I think they're all Catholic going back centuries.'

'But we all believe in God,' Angela said.

'Uh-huh. Did you see the accident? On the toboggan run?'

'I heard about it. It sounded terrible.'

'From après-ski to après-vie in two seconds flat.'

'Beverley, don't joke.'

'I'm not joking. I saw them. It shook me up so much I had to go get myself a drink.'

'You saw them? What was it like?'

'Red. Red and trying to scream.'

'I don't want to hear.'

67

You just want to ask about it, Beverley thought. She put down her coffee cup and said, 'Have you ever seen the ice maze?'

'Of course. It's fun, if you can get into it. All the kids want to play there. It's considered a children's thing.'

'But it must be dangerous, if it's ice.'

'They have these big pillows they ride on. About the size of a rubber raft. I haven't heard it's so dangerous. Want to try it?'

'Okay,' Beverley said. 'Just let me go to the ladies' room.'

The ladies' room, only one of several in the building, was as full as an airline lavatory of free gift-wrapped soaps, bottles of cream and eau-de-cologne. Beverley took one of everything.

They put on their outdoor clothes again and stepped out on to the long porch that ran the length of the lodge. Spectators sat in deck-chairs all along the railings. On the level above, indoors, there was an enclosed verandah for sunbathers, who lay basking behind glass walls and windows that let through the ultra-violet rays. There had been one year when the visitors had read magazine articles claiming that the ultra-violet was just the part of sunlight that caused skin cancers; and the number of sunbathers dropped dramatically. But the next year everyone had forgotten the scare. They wanted to be tanned again.

Beverley followed Angela. As she walked, she thought about how strange it was to be up where all the swish hotels were and the moneyed people who went to places like that only because they wanted to have rooms with a specific look, or a certain kind of food in the dining-room and dry martinis at the bar. She passed one woman, an American, who was shouting, 'Hector, Hector,' at someone; the woman wore dark glasses and a large mink coat. On her hands she displayed an array of massive gold rings set with stones bigger than eyes. Her fingernails were painted red and in her right hand she held a plastic coca-cola cup. Why leave America, Beverley wondered, if that was what you wanted?

Why had Angela left? Maybe they were people who just didn't believe the places where you took your vacation were part of the real world, especially if the native inhabitants spoke a different language.

They waited in line for two pillows and launched themselves into the ice maze, which was funnier and more exciting than Beverley had imagined, and less tiring than skiing. She sped forward through the glistening runways on her striped cushion and yelled as loudly as the children around her.

Afterwards they joined Angela's friends for sandwiches and coffee and then went out on the skating rink. When Beverley said she had to go, they begged her to stay on for tea and supper and dancing. There was a wonderful pool down inside the hotel, too. Beverley said no, she had to get back.

'But tomorrow?' Angela asked. 'Come on up tomorrow, or meet us early down at the Adler.'

'Maybe,' she said. She was sure Claus would want to be with her. She hurried as the light began to go. She was worried that he might have been waiting for a long time. But she was the first one back. When he came in, he was smiling, and in an even better mood than the day before. The slopes had been splendid, he told her: simply magnificent. Tomorrow he'd go even higher.

'Will you be all right with your friends?' he asked.

'I guess so.' She tried not to act hurt. They had a good dinner and a lot to drink, and went to bed as soon as they got back to their room.

He was up early and kissed her goodbye while she was still in bed. She set her alarm clock and went back to sleep.

For the next three days their separate daytime routines worked out well. He kept finding bigger and better ski runs up in the mountains, and she could tell him all about the hotel, the ice maze, the skating, the heated pool and the game rooms. She also told him that Angela, although she'd never mentioned it again, had confessed to being a member of some weird religious cult.

'As long as it isn't political,' he said.

'Those things never are.'

'Of course they are. What do you think?'

'Well, in this part of the world it wouldn't matter; only in the East, where they might start handing out Bibles or something.'

'What do they believe in?'

'She didn't say exactly, but the name is loony enough. I once had a terrible conversation with a couple of Seventh Day Adventists. I think that's what they were. It lasted three hours and twenty minutes. All this horrible stuff about being the elect. I couldn't get away. I didn't want to be rude. Jehovah's Witnesses, that's what it was.'

'Ridiculous. We used to get them at the door when I was in Cologne. You just tell them you're already something – Catholic, Jewish, Muslim – and say you believe in that.'

'But I don't. I didn't want to upset them, but I did finally say it didn't matter to me if I wasn't saved.'

'But you believe in God.'

'Of course,' she said. She had to say it because of the first time he'd asked her, in bed. 'Do you believe in God?' he'd whispered; and she had said yes, since she couldn't say anything else, and since what he was really asking her was: did she love him beyond anything. But later she was furious. It was as if in the throes of intercourse she had been asked, 'You do believe the sun goes around the earth, don't you?' What could you say? *Let me think about that one.* It was unfair.

He had been profoundly shocked when she'd told him that in accordance with her father's humanitarian principles, she had never been baptized. Her father had believed that people should wait until they were old enough to understand the words said over them, and could then choose whether or not they wanted to join a church.

Claus had said, 'But that's terrible. Every civilized human being – '

That was the point at which she had seen that despite his reputation in the hospitals as a rebel and a firebrand, he would always want to abide by the rules he'd grown up with, and that they included strictures of thought as well as of behaviour. When he reached up to push her hair away from her forehead, she'd pull a face and tell him, 'That makes such a bad impression,' or, 'What will the neighbours say?' She'd invented a quavery, shaking voice to quote his favourite scolding phrases back at him. But she'd kiss him afterwards.

'All this mystic nonsense that's supposed to be masquerading as a religion,' he said. 'I don't know how you can associate with them. I wouldn't want to be in the same room with people who are so stupid. Fanatics. Like being in the wards for the insane.'

'You thought they looked all right the other night.'

'Look, maybe. It's the ideas.'

'Do you think the idea of life after death is less peculiar than their plans to distribute sweetness and light?'

He talked for a long while about the ineradicable false romanticism of Americans. He said he thought it had something to do with not having lived through a wartime occupation recently, or even a war that had been fought over their territory.

She agreed with him, though she felt that since they were talking about her country, she should have been the one to criticize it. He didn't like it all that much when she had things to say against Germany; he'd tell her that her opinion was interesting but, as he'd go on to explain, somehow misinformed, if not just plain wrong: she hadn't been looking at something in the right way.

They had once had a terrible quarrel – which had gone on all night – about Germany's part in the Second World War. She had become genuinely hysterical, while he'd remained unconcerned. And after that she thought that although she couldn't live without him, she might not be able to stand being married to him. She wasn't really absolutely sure if she could stand being married to anyone: to end up like other married women who were full of recriminations, unfulfilled, nagging; and who spent their time cleaning and scrubbing and having children – all of which she'd come to eventually, of course, though at the moment the idea of such a future, such a fate, repelled her. Marriage was going to be the price of being allowed to stay with Claus.

'That hotel used to be a sanatorium,' he told her.

'I'm not surprised. I feel a lot better since I've been swimming in the pool.'

'Not that kind. For tuberculosis. A lot of famous people died there. Then they all moved to Switzerland.'

'After they died?'

'The famous people started going to Switzerland instead. And after that, people stopped getting TB so much.'

'The rich people stopped,' she said. 'They're giving a big party up there on New Year's Eve.'

'Let's stay down here. I don't want to be with a lot of other people.'

She didn't want to, either. She'd had enough of the crowds in the daytime – on the skating rink, in the ice maze, along the observation porches. She had also, temporarily, had enough of Angela's friend, Tom, who had taken her over on her second day at the ski lodge and insisted on sticking with her every minute, as if they had been a high school couple. She hadn't asked him about the religious movement, or about much else. He had kissed her in the hotel corridors between the tea-rooms and the swimming pool, and she had allowed it and kissed back even while she asked herself what she was doing in that group and why she should be letting him near her. She didn't want to have to explain about Claus. Maybe she wouldn't have to, anyway. She and Tom clung to each other against the hotel wallpaper and embraced. He knew how to kiss, all right, but in other ways seemed oddly incompetent. He was utterly lacking in the purposeful manipulations she was accustomed to from Claus. He seemed to be getting excited about her, but to be unwilling to follow through. She even wondered if he'd ever had a girl.

She also wondered why she should need this additional proof that she was desired. She knew that already. All the boys in Angela's circle approved of her. And she knew why:

it was because she had been another man's woman – that was all there was to it. She was prettier than she used to be, and she was a real woman, because of Claus. But Claus had had other affairs before her. She herself had never had anyone else. It put her at a disadvantage with him.

They stayed in their hotel for New Year's Eve. Only four other couples were in the dining-room. At midnight the lights were turned out and she kissed Claus in the dark. A local band was brought in, a crowd gathered, and people began to dance. Herr Lucas danced with an old woman who might have been his mother or perhaps his wife. Beverley and Claus swayed slowly over the polished but uneven floor. She was slightly drunk and sleepy and was happy thinking about how much she loved him, how wonderful he was, even the smell of his skin, which drove her crazy; and how everything had to turn out all right in spite of his horrible mother and all the things he didn't want to talk about because he was lazy and it was easier not to think about them if he didn't have to.

Next day, Angela said suddenly, 'Are you in love with this guy?'

Beverley was just biting into a sandwich. She nodded.

'Have you really thought about what it would be like to get married to a foreigner?'

'Um.'

'Would he fit in?'

'Oh, we'd live here.'

'Here?'

'In Europe. Well, that's where he works.'

'But – gee, I couldn't stand that. I mean, it's nice, but it's so different. You know.'

'That's why I like it.'

'But it isn't democratic.'

'Is America?'

'Of course. America is a democracy. Where did you go to school, Beverley?'

'For a couple of years, to the same place you did. And then,

73

I was at one of those liberal progressive numbers where you couldn't get in if you weren't the right kind. They used to take a certain per cent of stereotype misfits and minorities to cover themselves, but it was pretty exclusive. I'm glad of it, too. I got a good education. Weren't your other schools like that? Or did you sit next to the children of roadsweepers and ditchdiggers?'

'Oh, school. I didn't mean that. I meant the country, and the government.'

'Tell me about the Fountain of Light.'

Angela said, 'It's a lifelong dedication to an ideal, Beverley. It's a force of good in the world.'

'Is it open to everybody?'

Angela began to talk about the 'Movement', as she called it. Beverley kept a straight face, but only just. From what she could gather, the Fountain of Light wasn't exactly like the Clan, but they were pretty near it. Their favourite word for people who disagreed with them was 'degenerate'.

'What does that mean?' Beverley asked.

'Psychologically evil and immoral.'

'I thought it had something to do with not living up to your ancestors.'

'No, honey – it's people that can't live up to an ideal.'

'Why can't they?'

'Because they're too degenerate.'

'I see,' Beverley said. 'That explains it.'

She asked Tom on their way to the swimming pool, 'Do you think I'm degenerate?'

He said, 'How do you mean?'

'Aren't you one of the Fountains of Light?'

'Well, yes.'

'So, do you think I'm degenerate?'

He looked very serious and said, 'Let's put it like this: I think you've fallen into evil ways.'

Beverley burst out laughing. She had to steady herself against the wall.

'It isn't funny,' he said. 'It's a tragedy.'

'What's a tragedy?'

'You and that guy you're with. What do you think you're doing?'

She took a deep breath and thought of telling him precisely.

'You must know it's wrong,' he said.

'What's wrong?'

'Well, you aren't married to him, are you?'

'No, and I'm not married to you, either.'

'That's different.'

'Oh? Why do you hold me tight and keep kissing me – do you love me? Are you planning to marry me?'

'Yes,' he said.

She was so shocked that she couldn't answer. He took her by the elbow and drew her down the hallway. He put his arm around her and began to talk about the commitment to love and the commitment to God. She felt battered. She couldn't even argue back.

They reached the doors to the changing-rooms. She said, 'Even if I were free – '

'You are free,' he told her.

'No. I'm bound to him. And I love him.'

'You don't love him. If you'd loved him, you wouldn't have let me kiss you.'

'I guess that was just because I'm so degenerate,' she said.

'We'll talk about it some more tomorrow.'

After their swim, he went to join Mimi and Darell on the ski slopes. She lay down on a mattress in the sun room and fell asleep for a few minutes. She had decided not to return to the Miramar the next day.

* * *

When she woke up, she heard two women talking. They were sitting right nearby on the next two mattresses and were speaking English. She opened her eyes, but she was facing the other way. She was looking at a lot of extremely old men and women in bathing suits. In the past two days the hotel

75

had filled up with some very ancient tourists. It seemed strange that they should come just for New Year's Eve; probably it was for the healthy air more than the celebrations.

'I've told them: we've really got to improve the security,' one of the women said. 'Anybody can come up here now. Look at what happened last week.'

Something about the voice disturbed Beverley. She had the feeling she'd heard it before, but she couldn't remember where.

She turned her head and found herself looking up into a face she recognized. She said, 'Oh. Mrs Torrence,' and sat up.

The woman's head moved sharply. She was in her early eighties and she looked actually younger than Beverley seemed to recall, but it was the same woman: a friend of her grandmother, years ago, back in St Louis. Beverley remembered her from vacations there.

'Who?' Mrs Torrence said.

'Beverley. My grandmother was –'

'Oh, of course,' Mrs Torrence said. She smiled. She introduced Beverley to the other woman, a Mrs Dace, who had hair that was dyed red, although she appeared to be the same age as her companion. She smiled pleasantly at Beverley and asked if she was staying at the hotel.

'No, I'm down in one of the villages. This is out of my price range, I'm afraid.'

'Then you're all alone up here today?' Mrs Torrence said.

'I was with some friends till just a little while ago. We'll be meeting for tea as usual, and then I'll go on back down.'

'Oh, do join us for tea. We can show you the parts of the hotel you'd never see.' She turned to Mrs Dace and said, 'You remember giving little Alma the tour? This'll be just the same. Such fun to have some young faces around.'

Beverley didn't want to be impolite. She accepted the invitation. In fact, she was rather looking forward to seeing some of the private suites; they might be ones that retained the original nineteenth-century decor or, even better, have been remodelled in the more famous *art nouveau* designs. The two women would be treating her to the tea; that made a difference, too. And, in addition, she'd be able to avoid Tom.

'We can leave a message with your friends, if you like,' Mrs Torrence said.

Beverley wrote a note to say she'd run into someone from home. Mrs Dace levered herself off the mattress and took the folded paper away; she promised to find an envelope for it and leave it at the reception desk. Mrs Torrence began to tell a series of stories about St Louis in the old days when she and Beverley's grandmother were girls. Beverley was delighted. She'd been very fond of her grandmother.

After they'd changed, they took an elevator up to one of the higher floors. Mrs Dace asked to be called Minnie and Mrs Torrence said her name was Martha and she'd be angry now if Beverley used anything but her first name from that moment on. She took a gold key out of her alligator bag and fitted it into a door at the end of the hallway. Beverley would never have known that the door led anywhere – it looked from the front like another ordinary linen closet or a place where the hotel maids would keep brooms and mops and maybe some extra sheets. The key, on the other hand, could have been real gold: it was in the form of a winged nymph naked from the waist up; her legs became the part of the key that went into the lock.

'Here we are,' Martha said.

They stood in a hallway parallel to the one they had left. The ceiling was higher, the mouldings more elaborate, the carpets more opulent. Ahead of her Beverley saw gilding, parquetry, Venetian mirrors and fresh flowers that blossomed from vases set in scalloped niches along the walls. She looked hard at everything, hoarding details to present to Claus later on, when he was back from the skiing and they'd be lying with their arms around each other; she'd tell him stories as if she were a traveller who had returned from foreign journeys: first she'd been able to bring back part of the world that belonged to Angela, and now it would be the places inhabited by the very rich and – so it appeared – the old.

Martha gave a commanding sign with her right arm, leading onward. They entered an adjacent corridor and came to a bank of windows that looked out on a view of ice-covered crags and fir trees going down into a chasm; arched and fluted snowfields hung in roofed masses above them.

'Wonderful,' Beverley said. She thought Claus would love it too.

'You can only see it from this side,' Minnie told her. 'It's reserved for us.'

'Shh.' Martha put up a warning finger. 'Beverley will think we're bragging.'

Minnie lifted her hand to her face. She muttered, 'Oh. Of course.'

Martha led the way into her rooms and then out again, into Minnie's. Beverley was staggered by the apricot satin bedspreads, the green marble sunken baths, the black and silver chairs. They told her the names of the designers and walked her farther along the hallways to a tea-room that looked like the main salon of an ocean liner. Minnie and Martha waved to a few groups at other tables; the men made motions of bobbing to their feet as they bowed forward. All the people were old. There were about fifty of them in the huge room. Beverley wondered if it was like an old people's outing: if Minnie and Martha were members of some sort of exclusive club for five-star holidays. She also had for a moment a sudden sense of isolation and strangeness. If she could have thought of an excuse, she'd have asked to go back. She was almost ready to make something up, to say, 'Oh, I just remembered. . . .'

'We generally come in a bunch,' Martha said. 'We're all friends here.' She smiled and added, 'Old friends.'

Tea came, with both cakes and sandwiches. Beverley began to eat voraciously. She'd worked up a hunger again from the swimming. The two old women watched as if pleased to see someone with such a hearty young appetite.

They talked about the skating and the ice maze. Martha asked Beverley how long she was staying and she answered that it would be only two more days because her friend had to get back to work. 'And you?' she said, to keep the conversation going.

'Oh, we both live here most of the year now,' Martha answered. 'I guess you could say we've retired to the mountains. Took to the hills.'

Minnie tittered and said, 'Yes, you could say that.'

'Don't you miss St Louis?' Beverley asked.

'I really try', Martha told her, 'to live in the present as much as possible. I like reading the papers and looking at TV.'

'Well, you could do that at home. You could –' Beverley stopped. She had been about to say something that had to do with how difficult she found it to think of living in Europe for ever, not just for a while. She had been getting ready to talk about Claus and her family. Something had sidetracked her. She stared at her teacup. What was it? The feeling of isolation and uncertainty came over her again. She cleared her throat. And suddenly, she remembered: St Louis. In St Louis, ten years before, when she was just a child, she'd been to Martha Torrence's funeral.

She looked up.

'Yes, dear?' Martha said.

This time Beverley was deserted by her natural instinct to hide herself before she was certain what was going to happen. She was too surprised to cover up. 'Mrs Torrence –' she said.

'Martha.'

'In St Louis. I went to your funeral.'

'Yes.' Martha sat smiling at her. Minnie was looking away at a corner of the room.

'Yes?' Beverley repeated. She remembered Claus saying: *A lot of famous people died there.* She breathed in. She felt her comprehension slipping. The time passed. She sat in her chair for what seemed like ten minutes, until she knew how to go on. 'Was it something to do with the insurance?' she asked.

'How smart of you, Beverley.' Martha grinned. You could see that her teeth were the best money could buy; and her cosseted complexion also, helped by face-lifts, no doubt. Beverley thought: *She probably looks a lot better than I do at the moment.*

'Not exactly a swindle,' Martha confided, 'but shall we say: a conspiracy. I was very fortunate in my doctor – a man who was five years my senior, and what he didn't know about nursing homes wasn't worth knowing. It's rather a long story. Shall I tell you?'

'Yes, please,' Beverley said. Now she was intrigued and thrilled. Claus wouldn't mind her being late, once she'd explained why. *Wait till I tell people*, she thought, *that I had a long talk with a woman who died ten years ago.*

Martha glanced at Minnie, who picked up her cup and saucer and said, 'You'll excuse me, won't you? Now that you've started in on the explanation, I'll just go say hello to Herbie.' She toddled off to a table up against a palm tree by the wall.

* * *

Martha said, 'A friend of mine had a terrible thing happen to her once. She was in her late sixties and her children were all in their forties. She had grandchildren and two great-grandchildren. It was a large family. And Ida, my friend, started to lose her memory and repeat things and get confused all the time. The family thought it was premature senility. You can't blame them; what can you do except take the advice of the experts? And in Ida's case the experts said she was deteriorating fast and should be in a home. And that was that. The children were devastated, but there was no choice. They had her put away and they went through the whole legal business of transferring the house and the property and the money, and dividing it up as if she'd already died. She'd been declared *non compos*, you see. And she was, of course. It was all perfectly straightforward. Except for one thing – the nursing home she was in: they automatically gave their patients antibiotics. So, suddenly, eighteen months after the trouble started, Ida was completely normal again. She'd just had some strange kind of infection. Well, maybe you can imagine: she woke up into this imprisonment, not even knowing where she was – or why – and was told that her own family had committed her and taken away everything, even her great-grandparents' silver spoons. And when the doctors came around and discharged her – it wasn't easy, you know. So much in life is a matter of trust.'

'Yes,' Beverley said, 'it's one of the most important things.' She was thinking about Claus again, and their dissatisfaction over the Christmas presents. *We each choose for ourselves*, she thought. *But does either of us trust the other to choose for both? And that's what marriage has to be. There has to be that trust on both sides.*

Martha said, 'Ida's family loved her very much. It was all a tragic mistake, or rather, a misdiagnosis. But it got me thinking: sometimes people aren't much loved by their families. I started to sound out a few of my other friends and you'd be surprised, you really would be, at how many were honestly afraid of getting pushed down the stairs or handed the wrong medicine, or just scared to death. When you're old – you've got the experience, but if your eyesight starts to go, and your hearing, and you aren't so quick on your feet any more, then it's frightening to know that people who don't like you – who sometimes actually hate you – are just waiting for you to die off, the quicker the better. And you wonder how far they'd go.'

'But the medical profession is very careful about that kind of thing.'

'The medical profession can mess something up just as fast as anyone else.'

'I'm engaged to a doctor,' Beverley said.

'Then you'll know I'm right. They misplace the X-rays, they operate and leave the sponge in, sometimes a clamp too, they get the names switched around and cut open the wrong one, they bring mothers somebody else's baby to feed. Isn't that right?'

'All I meant was, if it's a matter of a person's sanity, so somebody else can get the money, then they're very careful.'

'So it seems. There are a lot of cases you don't read about because they never get to the papers. There are a lot of families who can't take it any longer. Ask a doctor in his seventies. They know. Anyway, about a dozen of us decided to do something. We formed a society. And now you've seen it.'

'You pretended to die, and got part of your money away first, and then you just came here?'

'That's right. We own this hotel and another one in Switzerland and a big place down in the Caribbean – we've got a whole island there – but the climate doesn't agree with everyone; it can be tough on arthritis sufferers. I really like it best here now. Of course, as far as the climate goes, we should really be based somewhere like Arizona, but that's too close to home for most of us. Too dangerous. We've got quite a big foreign contingent, but the majority of us are still American. There are a lot of us now, too. In ten years we've gotten up to about fifteen hundred. Quite a sizeable little club. And now you're one of us.'

'Don't worry,' Beverley laughed. 'Your secret's safe with me.'

'Of course it is. Because you'll be staying here. That's why I've been talking to you.'

'Staying? How do you mean?'

'You're going to be staying here now, with us. There's no other solution. It's what I was saying about the importance of trust, Beverley – we simply can't afford it. We've broken the law: just think of the tax situation for a start. And on top of that, we'd have the families after us. Impossible. You'll settle down soon. It can be very entertaining here, you know.'

Beverley sat back in her chair. She surveyed the people at the other tables, who, she could now see, were darting interested glances in her direction. But maybe she was imagining it. Maybe it was just because she was the one young person in the room. Or – because they all knew Martha Torrence went off the deep end like this whenever she found somebody new to talk to? Or maybe they were all in on it, and this could be some special refinement on a game they played with strangers and outsiders.

She decided to argue it through and find out how much more was to come. She said, 'Time is on my side.'

'That's true,' Martha admitted. 'In twenty years, I and all my friends will be dead – really dead. But the movement is very popular now. There are new recruits every year. And every year they're going to be just a little younger than me. Eventually, they'll be your age.'

Beverley tried to laugh, and couldn't. She wanted to get up and leave, but she knew she'd never find her way back through the corridors. And besides, she'd need the gold key. When she thought of the key, she felt sick. The picture came back to her with loathsome clarity: of the old woman's well-manicured hand clutching the winged, golden, naked girl and fitting the feet into the keyhole.

'There's nothing to worry about,' Martha said. 'We've got help from the outside. Maybe you've met some of them – the Fountain of Light movement?'

'What?'

'Of course, they're under the impression that they're fund-raising for other people. It wouldn't be right to tell them the truth. So many young people nowadays need to feel they're part of something grand and important. I don't think they'd appreciate being told that their efforts were really only keeping a large group of very self-indulgent great-grand-parents in the champagne and cigars of their choice. The young are so in love with ideals. They might not see the humour of it.'

This time Beverley did laugh. That would really be something to tell Claus; and her parents, too. She lifted her cup shakily, drank, and sloshed some of the tea into the saucer.

Martha continued, 'You'll be completely taken care of. You'll be our pet. I must say, it will be a delight to have a young face to look at. And our old boys will simply adore you. You'll be idolized.'

'I'd rather be loved;' Beverley said. 'Really loved.' Tears began to roll down her cheeks. 'I'd rather', she said, coming right out with it, 'be in bed with my boyfriend.'

'I daresay. But one can overcome that. There are other things in life. You'll just have to apply yourself to them.'

Beverley put her hand up to rub it across her face. She stared back at the inquisitive old people. 'What other things?' she said bleakly.

'Well, we could start off,' Martha told her cheerfully, 'by teaching you how to play bridge. Unless you already know how. You could join the tournaments. We've got some marvellous players here.'

'I'm pretty strong. I could escape.'

'Yes. Unfortunately that's what the others have always tried. They take someone into their confidence and then – it's distressing, but if it goes that far, we have to do something about all of them.'

For the first time Beverley believed the whole story. Her room down in the village, the skiers on the slopes, even the genuine guests on the other side of the hotel seemed as far away as if they existed in a different country. The key had gone into the lock and she was separated from the rest of life. 'The three people on the toboggan run?' she said.

'I'm afraid so.'

She thought back to the swimming pool: the artificial heat and light, Minnie and Martha talking. 'And little Alma?' she asked.

'Yes, her too.'

'Who was she?'

'She was the girl before you. You see, if you hadn't said anything about remembering my funeral – well, we'd have let you go. Even if you remembered later and told people about the hotel, no one would take you seriously. But your reaction was so strong.'

84

'I remembered the funeral because I went with my grandmother and I was worried about her. She died fairly soon after that. And I do remember that she cried like anything over you.'

'You mustn't be angry at me for that. My son-in-law was getting ready to have me certified for the sake of a few hundred thousand dollars. And my daughters would never have gone against him. Never.'

'Have you been happy here?'

'Blissfully happy. The peaceful nobility of the mountains – there's nothing like it. The food is delicious, the wonderful air – and we have the most fabulous doctors, of course; the hot springs and the sun rooms: I'm talking now about our own facilities on this side of the building. We only cross over, we only really come out at all, at New Year's, to see all the young people. That's the only thing we miss.'

'I'd miss it even more than you would,' Beverley cried. 'Couldn't you take my word for it that I wouldn't ever tell anybody?'

'We can't. We just can't. You've got to see that. No, dear, it's much too good a story. You could even sell it for money to the papers. I'm afraid not. You'll have to get used to it. Don't look to the others for help – they're a lot stricter about the rules than I am. You just relax now, and accept. I think you'll find it's going to be in your interest to adopt a pleasant and friendly attitude. Try to breathe in the spirit of serenity that these wonderful mountains induce.'

When she didn't come back, Claus would try to find her. He'd telephone the Miramar; he'd go down to the Adler to look up Angela and her friends. After that, he'd go to the police. Perhaps that would be the moment for an eminently respectable and distinguished-looking elderly couple to step forward and say, 'We saw her heading down the mountain just as it was getting dark. She didn't seem to know how to ski very well and she took the most difficult route.' Then the search parties would spread out over the snow, Claus among the number. But no one would really be surprised if her

85

corpse couldn't be found. People disappeared all the time in the mountains, all year long. The mountains were like the oceans in that respect – every season was deadly.

'We aren't even in the danger zone for avalanches,' Martha said. 'Anyway, long before the unstable periods, the men get out and fire things off to loosen the snow and send it in the right direction. We're well protected in every way.' She bent forward, took Beverley's arm and stood up. 'You just come on over here,' she ordered, 'and sit down.'

Beverley rose unsteadily. She felt as dazed as if the tea they'd been drinking had been drugged. Once more tears ran over her face. She allowed herself to be steered to the small table where Minnie was talking with an old man. The man stood and bowed as they approached. Martha pushed her gently into the third chair and sat next to her.

Beverley sniffled and raised the back of her hand to her eyes. The old man held out a handkerchief to her, which – after a hesitation – she took. She thought miserably that it was no wonder the other young ones they'd held prisoner had been willing to risk escape, if not to take the risk meant year after year, for ever: never in her life to see Claus again, or to get back home, to see her family; her body and her life unused and unknown.

'Are you ready?' Martha asked. 'Good. Now try to remember: the most important thing to get straight about bridge is the bidding.'

BLESSED ART THOU

Brother Anselm had come into the chapel early. He seemed to want to confess. Brother Francis had gone to the confessional and waited, but nothing had happened. When he'd come out to look, Anselm was in the covered archway, pacing to and fro; he was making vestigial, instantly repressed explanatory gestures in the air and occasionally he'd turn his head towards the square of green grass beyond the stone pillars, though he didn't appear to be taking it in.

Francis became interested. It was rare to see such signs of distress in a brother; ever since the new permissiveness, most people had become too good at dissembling. His friend, Frederick, who ran the place, had clamped down so hard on all unusual behaviour that from being a recently liberated enclosed order they had become practically suffocated by stricture. And this reaction against licence had actually forced them into a departure from tradition. Francis realized that. He would never have said so to Frederick. Their monastery was definitely a one-man show. It always had been and remained so even now, when Frederick was only the acting head. At times Francis thought of himself as the First Mate and of Brother Adrian as the Second Mate. Frederick stood indisputably at the helm.

Francis and Frederick had been through so much together that they were like old soldiers; each had sustained the other through more than one crisis of faith. They could speak their doubts and not have the words taken the wrong way. They knew their faults and still liked each other. Neither one of them was so sure that they liked Brother Adrian very much, though they certainly knew his faults, too. Brother Adrian was short, meaty, red-faced and opinionated. He was sometimes right, but right or wrong, always at loggerheads with Frederick, who was a tall, elegant, ironic man often prone to outbursts of ferocious rudeness, bad temper and bigotry. Brother Francis was the peacemaker. He recognized the important fact that both men had faith. He knew in his heart that that would overcome all obstacles.

But there was no doubt that for the past four years life had been monotonous in the order: dull and without flavour. He had even heard young Brother William say to his friend, Elmo, that violence was not necessarily to be deprecated, as sometimes it 'cleared the air', a sentiment for which he had been reprimanded. And when the rebuke had been administered, the boy had made everyone gasp by asking, 'Is Brother Francis going to be censured for eavesdropping?' That was the last scandal they had had – two months ago. All wounded feelings had now healed. William had even admitted that he had been more or less shouting at the time. And life had returned to the uneventful rules and routines. So, it was intriguing to see Anselm displaying such uncustomary agitation.

Francis watched for a while without showing himself. He was pretty sure that Anselm wouldn't go away until he'd made some kind of decision. He began to feel more and more curious as he watched.

He was patient. He knew that Anselm was a serious young man who liked to think things over for a long time before committing himself to an opinion. His faith was divided; his approach to God was intellectual and therefore in constant danger of attack by itself. He was twenty-seven, had dark hair and dark eyes, and was nice-looking but nervy. He sometimes talked too fast. When he had the feeling that he wasn't getting through to people, or that his ideas would escape if he didn't put them into words – it was like a panic, he'd said to Francis: there was always a right moment, and you could miss it.

The order was fortunate in having so many young men. Elmo and William were in their early twenties, James and Duncan in their thirties. Just at the time when the young ones had rushed from the open doors of other monasteries, theirs had received recruits. Frederick had said sourly that there would always be some who found relief in seeking out suffering for a while. But their young ones had stayed. They hadn't all had an easy time. Francis had felt so sorry for them that in his own recurrent crises of faith they had nearly caused him to despair. There had been one terrible, long night when he'd been roaring drunk, saying it was a crime to inflict mental torture on the young; Frederick had had to hold his head while he was sick.

* * *

Anselm stalked past the stone columns, the green wedges of grass showing between. 'Father,' he muttered, 'I have . . . that is to say, you aren't going to believe this, but. . . .'

At last he came to a stop and sat down with his back against one of the pillars. He longed for a cigarette, but he'd given them up six years before. He shut his eyes, opened them again on the picture of stone archways, grey skies and grass, and sighed.

It had been just like this, but a wonderful day, not overcast like today: a time taken out of a milder season – springlike, marvellously full of sunshine, the sky blue as if enamelled, the air warm. And he was on the other side of the building, just like this, when he wasn't supposed to be – he'd just skipped his duties and routines and thought somebody could go ahead and report him: he didn't care. And nobody had reported him, either, which was also strange, but of course it was nothing compared to what was to come, because – he was looking out, like this, into the warm, grassy courtyard and when he'd lifted his face to the bright air there had been a loud, rapid fluttering sound, a heavy thump, and there in front of him on the expanse of green was a handsome young man, stark naked and smiling. Behind him, quivering and drawing themselves inward, were two large wings made of what appeared to be golden feathers. As Anselm watched, they pleated together and disappeared, leaving – so he was later to discover – no bodily trace on their owner. The young man looked right at him. He was still smiling. He took a step forward and held his arms out.

Anselm knew straight away that this was the friend he'd been hoping for all his life. He had made a mistake to think that he could look deep into his own spirit and find a new and better self; the elusive other self was already inhabiting someone else. Only by loving another person did you find that part of yourself.

He moved forward, opening his own arms, falling into the waiting embrace. The young man kissed him on the cheek, on the neck, on the mouth; hugged him, stroked and patted him lightly, and started to undo his clothes. Anselm was fairly certain that there was no one around at the moment, but there might be one other person who, like him, had decided not to do what he'd been ordered to that day; so he told the young man, breathlessly, that they'd better go to his cell. He pulled him quickly across the sunny grass, into the dark stone archways and corridors, to his tiny room. He closed the door.

The young man removed the rest of Anselm's clothes and fell on the bed with him. He seemed to be shedding light from his nakedness into all parts of the room. Anselm could hardly breathe. He knew what was happening but he couldn't quite connect it with anything else. He supposed it was really only the kind of thing he'd been warned about all his childhood: they tried to do it to you in washrooms, everyone had told him. And the Church frowned on it. Of course he'd somehow suspected it must be fun, otherwise people wouldn't be so much against it, but all the same, he wasn't prepared for this: to be touched all over, lovingly and thoroughly, in every kind of way, as he'd always – though he knew it was wicked – dreamed it would be like to make love. He was very nervous, but he was overjoyed.

He kept his head enough to ask the man's name afterwards. 'Gabriel,' his friend told him. Anselm fell asleep in his arms. When he woke, Gabriel had gone.

Anselm got up and dressed, walked back to the courtyard and looked around. He thought he could detect some indentations in the grass that might have been made by the pressure of the angel's feet as he'd taken off.

He expected Gabriel to meet him at the same hour the next day. He rushed to the place long before it was time and waited, his eyes devouring every inch of his surroundings in an excess of anticipation. But Gabriel didn't return.

Anselm waited the next day too, and was again disappointed. He began to feel desperate. He couldn't eat. He didn't think he was going to be able to live through the next day. But he still believed that Gabriel would come back.

Three different people criticized him for neglecting his duties. Although usually he was so overly diligent that he'd have been thrown into consternation by any expression of disapprobation, now he really didn't mind. Waiting for Gabriel was more important. He actually told the most persistent of his critics to shut up and mind his own business.

By the end of the week he knew that it was over. Gabriel wasn't going to come back. It had been a single visitation: not to be repeated.

He realized that he had never before known what it was to suffer. The pain of trying to accept the loss of love was too much for him. He felt himself beginning to break up, to become confused; he couldn't remember things, he couldn't keep his attention on anyone. He had to talk to somebody.

The only person he could think of was Brother Francis, who was usually understanding and kind, and got along with everyone.

He should go to Brother Francis and confess. He knew that; he was ready to do it. Not until he was outside the chapel did it strike him that it wasn't going to be that easy to begin. He worked himself into such a state that by the time he finally entered, his head was down and his arms hanging. He shuffled towards the confessional.

Francis nipped in at the other end.

Anselm stared into the darkness and sighed. He said, 'I don't know how to put it.'

'It's all right, Anselm,' Francis told him. 'Just make a beginning somewhere. Have you sinned?'

'And how.'

'I beg your pardon?'

'All over,' Anselm babbled, 'kissing and touching – it was wonderful, lovely. It was so delightful, and I know it's a sin, but it's the only truly magical thing that's ever happened to me – right out of this world. I'm not sorry about it. All I can think of is how much I want it to happen again. But every time I go there and wait for him, I know it's the end; he isn't coming back. And I can't stand it. I just don't know what to do now. It's so lonely. It's killing me, Francis. What am I going to do?'

'Anselm, you know we're supposed to give up all – all – all that sort of thing.'

'I didn't have to give it up – I never had it. No, never before. And maybe they're right about the other kind; I don't know. But this was wonderful. The feeling of joy – and it didn't leave me afterwards. It grew. I felt transformed. I knew I should confess it, but it was like a secret he'd trusted me with. And after all, he takes precedence, doesn't he?'

Brother Francis forgot the rules. 'This is appalling,' he said.

'The only really sublime, magnificent thing that's ever happened to me. An angel – an angel from heaven, coming down to earth. But now he's gone, I feel so sad. I miss him. I can't tell you how much I – all day long, all the time, all . . .' Anselm started to cry.

Francis knew that he shouldn't say anything more without consulting someone, but he couldn't remain silent while his fellow man suffered. 'It's all right,' he said. He got up from his seat, went around to haul Anselm out into the light, and made him sit down in one of the pews. Anselm leaned forward, his head against his hands and his hands gripping the edge of the pew in front of him. Francis patted him on the back and repeated that it was all right. 'Who did you say this other young man was?' he asked.

'Gabriel.'

'I can't recall a Brother Gabriel in the order.'

'He's an angel. I told you. He came – he just landed, and folded up his wings.'

'Wings?'

'I still remember the joyfulness, but how can anything be the same again? It was amazing the way he appeared, out of nowhere. And now ordinary life isn't any good. It feels unliveable.'

'Wings?' Francis said again.

'Golden wings. The real thing.' Anselm's voice sounded choked and tearful. He slumped forward on to the floor. He seemed to have fainted. Francis pulled him up. He told him to go back to his cell and lie down, and that he'd send Duncan to him.

'I don't need a doctor,' Anselm said, but he went back to his cell obediently, lay down and fell asleep.

*　　*　　*

Francis was worried. He went to see Frederick. 'I think something's wrong with Anselm,' he said, and told him the story.

'Should you be telling me this?' Frederick asked.

'Consider it a confession. I don't know what to do.'

'That's simple. We find the joker and throw him out.'

'Who?'

'The gardener's boy? Damn it, you can't tell about anyone any more. He looked perfectly harmless to me. A little drip that could barely put one foot in front of the other.'

'Exactly. Definitely not the type. Not like the last one.'

'Yes, well. A heavy drinker, but marvellous with the bulbs. I suppose we'd better just wait till Anselm pulls himself together.'

'He said it was an angel. With wings. Golden wings.'

'I see. Have you asked Duncan to take a look at him?'

'He won't see Duncan.'

Anselm went back to his ordinary life. He didn't speak to

93

anyone else about his visitation, but somehow word ran around the monastery that he had seen an angel in a vision. People began to come to his cell to ask him about it. He told them all the same thing: 'I don't want to talk about it.' But the higher powers became alarmed by this evidence of interest.

They called Anselm before them. He sat in a chair facing Frederick, Francis and Adrian.

Frederick said, 'All right, Anselm. Tell us about it.'

'It's just what I said to Francis,' Anselm mumbled. 'I don't think it should be anyone else's business. I'm trying to get used to it.'

'I'm sorry, Anselm,' Francis said. 'This is only because the others have been talking.'

'Oh, it isn't you. I don't blame you.'

'Who do you blame, then?' Brother Adrian said.

'Who do you? Why am I here?'

'Delusion.'

'You think it was an optical illusion?'

'Delusion. Delusions of grandeur. *I did it with angels.*'

'Only one.'

'Or', Frederick said, 'could it have been a man? Someone in the order, for example?'

'No.'

'These things sometimes occur, regrettable though they may be.'

'Who regrets it?'

'Who was it, Anselm?'

'I've told you. And you don't believe it. All right, never mind. May I go now?'

'Let's be more specific about what actually happened.'

'I do not propose to discuss what went on between us.'

'You don't have to. I can imagine it well enough. That wasn't what I had in mind. What I'm trying to ascertain is whether at any stage during this alleged encounter the wings got in the way.'

'I've said already: they'd disappeared.'

'Where to?'

'Inside.'

'Inside? How?'

'Well, I'm not sure. When I saw it happen, he was facing me. I guess they must be like those fold-up umbrellas you can get: you know, sort of collapsible. When you don't need them, you can – '

'Anselm, this joke has gone far enough. Come on, now. What's going on? You're feeling the need of drama and eventfulness here?'

'A lack of attention?' Adrian added. 'But you didn't join our order for that, did you?'

'I joined it because I love God. And now, at last, I've got the proof that He loves me back. He sent His angel to me and showed me. You say you can imagine, but you can't. You just can't. It was a pleasure beyond anything.'

'Oh, Christ,' Frederick muttered.

'And he was beautiful.'

'A figment of the – '

'I felt like a tree,' Anselm said wildly. 'A barren tree that's come into flower for the first time.'

'That's rather vague,' Francis said. 'What happened?'

'Well, after he took off my clothes, we sort of fell on to the bed and – '

'Please,' said Frederick. 'Spare us the details.'

'Francis asked what happened.'

'This is so sordid,' Adrian murmured.

Anselm exploded. 'How dare you?' he yelled. 'How dare you say that about any of God's creatures, much less an angel? We are not sordid. We're good. God made us and God loves us the way we are, even if we don't always do everything right.' He burst into tears. 'I can't go on,' he sobbed.

Francis made a move to rise and go to him, but Frederick held up his hand. Anselm fought for control. He began to calm down.

'I think you should have a talk with Brother Duncan,' Frederick told him.

'I'm all right now. I just got upset.'

Adrian said, 'You can claim you saw this, and you can claim you saw that, but the fact remains that nobody else saw – '

Anselm turned his head. 'You weren't chosen,' he sneered. 'I was. And', he said defiantly, 'his skin was like honey.'

'That's enough of that,' Frederick said. 'I'm ending this interview now. Anselm, if you won't agree to talk to Brother Duncan, you'll have to consider yourself confined to quarters until further notice.'

*   *   *

The incarceration was intended to be a punishment, but it also showed that they were afraid he might get out. Why would he want to do that? He lay on his bed – on the same bed where it had all taken place, and where he could remember if he shut his eyes or even lowered the lids a little – and tried to figure out why they were so worried. From their point of view, of course, he'd just been seeing things. Most closed communities were stiff with people who hadn't been able to stand the strain; even if they didn't crack, it was uncommon to find more than half of them without some kind of fissure. But they stayed, naturally. The world outside was so much worse. He himself, as they knew, had sought out the order as a refuge – a solution. And now it was where the best thing of his life had happened to him. It didn't make sense that he should want to leave, yet they were afraid. He started to feel apprehensive about their fear.

At the other end of the building from his cell, the senior brothers argued. 'You're making him a martyr,' Francis said. 'That's just what so many of the young ones want: the glory and romance of the persecuted believer.'

'He isn't all that young,' Frederick said. 'Nearly twenty-seven. That stuff's for the teenagers.'

'Haven't you noticed how the rest of them are taking his side against you?'

'Against us.'

'Except Adrian. That's a surprise. I never thought he'd agree with you on anything. I think he's just set against the poetry of it. He doesn't think other men, especially young ones, should have such fancy ideas.'

'Francis, it's the question of the morality that's so repulsive.'

'Yes, I'm not very fond of morals myself.'

'The lust, Francis. The gross flagrancy of the sexual intercourse. The immorality in any case, but in this case much more so. The perversion, for heaven's sake.'

'Perhaps.'

'Definitely.'

'I hope you and Adrian will take into account my firm conviction that it's necessary for people to be able to have their dreams. For the young, it's essential. And in a place like this, there's almost no other way to express the more flamboyant aspects of their nature. Do you understand?'

'I guess so. But it's the others I'm concerned about.'

'The others think it's too harsh to shut him away for a harmless fantasy. He didn't need to talk about it, after all.'

'Oh, talking about it was the point. You don't think all that big, lush story of kisses and touching would have been half as good without other people's reactions, do you?'

'He's always been a good boy, and conscientious. A bit serious and moody, a bit frightened of other people. But spiritually sound, Frederick. His heart's in the right place, I think.'

'It wasn't his heart he was boasting about.'

'He wasn't boasting. He was in distress.'

'Boasting. Adrian was right about that. "I was chosen," he said. And so on.'

'I just think, to be so severe – it might not be the right way to handle it.'

'One more week. Then we'll have another talk with him.'

*   *   *

Anselm let himself dream. He lowered his eyelids and remembered. He was happy, even though he didn't think

97

it was very healthy to be cooped up the way he was. He did exercises in the cramped space, but they didn't seem to help much. He had pains in his chest. He lost interest in his theological texts. He yearned for things he'd left long ago – for instance, he'd have liked to see a really exciting movie full of car chases. It took him a long while to recover from his night's sleep. He didn't seem to wake up so quickly or so fully as usual, and the morning meal of lumpy porridge and tough old wheatmeal bread made him feel nauseated.

At last the brother who brought the food came to say that the sentence was up. The man's name was Dominic and he'd been dying of curiosity all the time he'd been coming to the cell. He had tried to sound Anselm out but had got no response, so when anyone asked him about his prisoner, he'd invent something. He made up anything he thought might be interesting, though nothing malicious; he said that one evening a bright light had seemed to be coming from under the door – brighter than could be accounted for by the ordinary lighting system available to the brothers; that kind of thing. By the time he unlocked the door and left it ajar, there was a fairly large corpus of mythological incident circulating through the monastery. He waited by the door, smiled widely and said, 'No more restrictions.'

Anselm stood up. He nodded.

Dominic said, 'Good heavens, they must really trust your sanity. I've never known them to allow anyone else in solitary to keep a razor.'

Anselm touched his cheeks and chin. He nodded again and walked from the room.

He went back to the cloister, where he strolled up and down to stretch his legs. He also needed to think. He paced back and forth in front of his favourite tree, a pear tree, which had come into bud while he'd been shut indoors, and would soon be in flower. Things were no longer simple; or, if they were, then they were so simple that nobody else was going to be able to agree with him.

He went to eat lunch with the others. He sat down late. The brothers had already joined in silent prayer. When the talk began again, heads turned towards him. The bread was passed around. Brother Adrian said loudly, 'You need a haircut, Anselm. See Brother Marcus after lunch. Did you hear me?'

Anselm ignored him. He looked down the table to where the doctor sat, and said, 'Brother Duncan, if it won't be disturbing you, I'd like to talk to you after the meal.'

'Did you hear me?' Adrian bellowed.

A silence fell over the company. Anselm murmured, 'How could anyone at this table fail to hear you, Brother Adrian? You're shouting so loudly. I'm perfectly capable of dealing with my hair, just as you must be of looking after what's left of yours.'

The roar of laughter from his companions turned Adrian red. He tried to stand up. The two brothers at his side held on to him.

Francis said, 'Argumentation is detrimental to the digestion, brothers. We all know that. Let's have some ideas and opinions on the new wines, all right?'

'They haven't settled down yet,' Brother Robert said. 'It's unfair to judge them at this stage.'

Everyone waited for Brother Robert to say more. He had a flair for the possibilities of a wine. He was a prematurely dried-up, pernickety little man, not the sort of person anyone would take to be an expert on a matter concerning the senses. He could drink huge amounts and, since the effect was to make him progressively quieter, he never seemed to be drunk – unlike Brother Adrian, who pontificated loudly and slurred very early on during the wine-tasting examinations and thought everything tasted pretty good.

'But just at a guess, Robert?' Francis asked. 'Good or bad?'

'Oh, the red is probably going to be ordinary enough. Drinkable, that's all. But the white could conceivably turn out to be something rather special for a California wine. Don't quote me. That's just off the top of my tonsure, ha-ha.'

99

Two of the brothers groaned. Brother William, one of the youngest, said, 'I thought the order hadn't had tonsures since Father Clement's time. I thought those were all just natural.'

'Go back to sleep,' his friend James told him.

'I wasn't asleep. I was thinking about something I wanted to ask Anselm, but now I've forgotten.'

Anselm glanced in William's direction. William twisted around in his seat and stared back. He looked baffled. He said, 'I just can't remember.'

Brother Adrian thundered down the table at Robert that the red wine this year was going to be full-bodied and rich as a ruby, not like the usual cat's piss the white wine drinkers were addicted to.

Most of the table joined in the quarrel. Since the entire monastery was divided into lovers of white wine and lovers of red, the subject was normally a guarantee for heated debate.

Anselm didn't take part. He chewed his food slowly, watched by the doctor from the other side of the table.

* * *

'Well, Anselm, what can I do for you?' Duncan asked. 'Feeling nervous again? Depressed? Having dreams?'

'I've always had dreams, Doctor. Haven't you?'

'Of course. The thing to remember about dreams is that you shouldn't let them run away with you.'

'I heard from somebody once that your great dream was to be a missionary doctor, like Albert Schweitzer. Is that true?'

'That's right, yes. What good memories people have around here. We all have our fantasies when we're young.'

'You're still not too old to do it.'

Duncan pointed to his heart. He said, 'I'm too old here.'

'So, if it was offered to you, you wouldn't accept?'

'Probably not. How did we get on to this? I was supposed to be asking you about your health.'

'I'm not sure that what I've got is really a matter of health.'

'You look different. Were you eating all right, the past few weeks?'

'Feel my cheek, Doctor,' Anselm said.

Duncan put out his hand and touched the side of Anselm's face. 'What's wrong?' he said. 'It doesn't feel like a temperature to me.'

'No beard,' Anselm explained. 'My beard has disappeared. It's just gone.'

Duncan hitched his chair closer. He took Anselm's face between his hands and turned it, first one way, then another. 'That's certainly what it looks like,' he said.

'And other things,' Anselm continued, 'have disappeared.'

'Oh?'

'And I'm getting fat. And I'd like you to take a look at my chest.' He stood up, turned his back, unsnapped the front of his robe and took out a towel he'd kept folded there. Then he turned around, holding the robe open so that the doctor could see: two round, exuberantly forward-pointing breasts, each about the size of a pomegranate.

Brother Duncan stood up. His mouth opened. He held out his hands as if to touch the breasts. Anselm picked up the towel and closed his robe. He sat down in the chair again.

The doctor continued to stare. At last he said, 'What the hell? Who are you?'

'I'm Anselm. You know very well. I've been in solitary confinement for a long time, so you know I couldn't have been switched. Maybe you heard something about the reason why they put me there?'

Duncan sat down. Once more he examined Anselm's face. 'I can't understand it,' he said.

'It isn't hard to understand, only hard to believe. I'm pregnant, that's all.'

'Right. Get your clothes off. All of them. This time I'm going to give you a complete examination.'

'Not on your life. I don't see why I should be subjected to any such thing without another woman present.'

'I'm a doctor.'

'Does that make you better than anyone else?'

'This is my job, Anselm.'

'But how much do you know about women?'

'I had a thorough medical education.'

'Exactly. That means: not much.'

'For Christ's sake, what do you think I'm going to do to you? I just want to look.'

'I bet. You can give me a urine test and find out that way.'

'Anselm, you don't seem to be taking this very seriously.'

'I'm taking it the only way that makes sense. I was chosen, and I accept it, and I'm glad. It's only everybody else who finds trouble in taking it. First of all they said I was crazy and seeing things. What are they going to say now?'

'Well, if it's true, how long do you think you can keep it secret? There's going to come a time when it'll start to show.'

'It shows already, without the towel.'

'Well, everybody's got to know pretty soon, then. Unless you're planning to leave here.'

'No, I couldn't leave. Doctor, you know that's what's happened, don't you? You know it's a sacred thing. And you're bound by your oath to preserve life. You're also pledged to keep my confidence.'

'I can keep quiet. But in your condition, you'll give yourself away. Don't you think it would be better if I examined you now, and after that we could both go to Brother Frederick and have a chat?'

Anselm yawned. He said, 'I suppose so. But I'm relying on you. If they shut me up again, I won't be able to get the exercise I need. It wouldn't be healthy. If you really need to, I guess you can do an examination. But I'm warning you: try anything dirty, and I'll knock your teeth out.'

'This is what holiness has done for you, is it? Talking to me like that.'

'I've been put in a position of trust. My body is a sepulchre. It shouldn't be tampered with.'

'Relax. I'm not going to tamper. I'm going to palpate.'

'That sounds worse.'

102

'Anselm – '

'Oh, all right,' Anselm said. He began to pull furiously at his clothes to get them off. He found that tears were running from his eyes. He cried easily now and got irritated, and felt sleepy during the daytime. 'And my back hurts,' he said.

* * *

'There's no doubt about it,' Brother Duncan said. 'Anselm is expecting a child. Physically, he is now in every respect a woman.'

Anselm leaned back in Frederick's easy-chair. He had positioned the pillow so that it would give support at the small of his back. The pregnant belly loomed out in silhouette. His hair was brushed back and seemed much longer; the style made his face look like a woman's.

It took a while for Frederick, Francis and Adrian to digest the news. In the end, Frederick had to bring out the brandy. Anselm alone refused.

'Oh dear,' Brother Francis said, 'oh dear, oh dear.'

Brother Frederick looked the doctor in the eye and told him, 'It just isn't possible.'

'Who knows? Darwin wasn't wrong about everything. Eels are sexually ambivalent, and snails are both male and female at the same time; but maybe they weren't always that way. Maybe they became like that after being some other way for a long time. Do you see what I mean? Maybe Anselm is only the first. He's evolved, so that – '

'No,' Anselm interrupted. 'I was chosen.'

'Perhaps mind over matter,' Francis said tentatively. 'If the desire was so strong. I'm not saying that it's psychosomatic, but . . . I don't know.'

'Yes,' Anselm said. 'I know what you mean. Love conquers all. I know that's true now. I've had the proof. In fact, I am the proof.'

Brother Adrian looked at Anselm with revulsion. He declared, 'It isn't in the realm of nature.'

103

'Nature covers a lot of territory. And it's changing all the time.'

'You know what I think we should do, Anselm? I think we should bring back the old practices and burn you at the stake.'

'Oh dear,' Francis said. 'Calm down, Adrian, please.'

'If it's a question of the survival of the Church?'

'But this is Anselm. We've known him for five years. He's a good boy.'

'He must have been a plant. By evil forces. Who knows what really went on? We have no idea.'

'I told you,' Anselm said.

'That's what I mean. The depths of sexual depravity.'

'It doesn't have anything to do with morality. It's all a question of love. I was given the love and it transformed me. And now that it turns out I've been given something else, that's going to be a wonderful reminder of –'

'Stop,' Frederick said. 'This is ludicrous.'

'Monstrous,' Adrian said. 'This progeny, whatever you want to call it, has got to be a monster. You're a living blasphemy, Anselm.'

'Don't say that.' Anselm took out a handkerchief and dabbed at his eyes.

'He's a medical anomaly, that's all,' Duncan said.

'This is not a miracle,' Adrian insisted. 'It's an abnormality. Brother Anselm is a freak, not a phenomenon.'

'Oh, you nasty man,' Anselm said, sniffing into his handkerchief.

'Yes, Adrian, really,' Francis said. 'Have a little compassion. In his state – after all, we don't want to upset the baby.'

'Baby? I wouldn't be surprised if it turns out to be a toad.'

'Gabriel,' Anselm whispered. He hid his face in the crook of his elbow. Francis patted his back and gripped his shoulder.

Frederick rose from his chair. He said, 'Well, Anselm, we'll just have to wait and see what you produce. In the meantime, I hope I don't have to tell you that no word of this is to leak out of the building. And while you remain here, you're to conduct yourself with modesty and decorum. That will be all for the moment. You may return to your cell. Perhaps you'd accompany him, Doctor? Him, her, whatever you want to call yourself.'

Anselm stood. 'God forgive you,' he said. He turned towards the door. Duncan took his arm. Brother Adrian shouted after them that Anselm would burn in hell for ever and ever.

Anselm let himself be led quietly to his cell. He lay down on his back and closed his eyes. He knew that he should try to think of some plan, some way of protecting himself. There were malicious and unscrupulous men around him, who despised him and who would have him at their mercy when the baby was born. He couldn't decide whether telling the outside world would help him or put him into greater danger.

He thought about the baby and smiled. He was feeling good in spite of the backaches. He fell asleep smiling.

* * *

Frederick went to Francis for comfort. He said, 'Francis, this thing will be the end of me. I don't know what to do. I can't tell anyone outside. On the other hand – I mean, it couldn't be. It couldn't be. You don't believe it, do you?'

'Well, the trouble is, we all know that he was a man when he arrived here.'

Frederick paced the room, smacked his hands together and pulled at his hair. He kept repeating that it wasn't possible.

'But it's happened,' Francis said.

'Okay, okay. What I meant was: it isn't possible that it could be another divine birth. In which case, in which – you aren't helping, Francis.'

'In which case, it's an ordinary human birth.'

'Yes. A phantom pregnancy brought on by Anselm's overwhelming neurotic craving to become the object of his devotion: the Virgin Mary.'

'And when he gives birth?'

105

'It's all going to be gristle and leftover pieces of stuff.'

'Frederick, sit down for heaven's sake. You heard what Duncan said. It's going to be a child like any other child.'

'Then he was screwing somebody in my monastery, damn it all.'

'As a man or as a woman?'

'Oh, Christ,' Frederick said. 'Years clawing my way up the ladder, being polite to creeps and crazies, and playing along with the whole business: you do me a favour, I'll do you a favour. And then I got my own team and whipped it into shape. I worked like hell on this place, you know that. Not that they'd actually let me have it for my own – no, I'm only the deputy; that makes it less trouble for them. And now this happens.'

'But no matter what's caused it, it's a joyful thing.'

'Not for the man in charge, Francis. No, siree. What the hell am I going to do?'

'All these emotions – it's wearing me down. Try to relax and be happy. Don't work yourself up like this.'

'Easy for you to say. You aren't going to have to carry the can.'

'Neither are you. Nobody's going to blame you for this. Especially if you call in Duncan to explain the situation.'

'He doesn't have an explanation.'

'That's just it. What you do is what everyone else is going to do: wait and see.'

'No. We believe in God, the Virgin Birth, Christ The Redeemer, the teachings of Mother Church and the life everlasting. And that's damn well it. None of this newfangled nonsense. And don't start quoting Vatican Two at me – I'm sick to death of it.'

'But you wouldn't do anything to harm Anselm, would you?'

'How are we to know that this isn't some kind of unholy thing? That's what Adrian believes.'

'The man's a fool, you know that. He's jealous of Anselm and he's frightened of his own feelings. Forget what he believes. Let's say for the moment that we're dealing with an ordinary mother and child. It would be very wrong to do anything to harm them.'

'I wasn't thinking of harming anyone. Don't look at me like that.'

'You tell me what you were thinking about, then.'

'I don't know. There doesn't seem to be any way out. Why did this have to happen to me?'

'It didn't. It happened to Anselm.'

'But it affects us all. No man is an island.'

'And no woman, either.'

Frederick jumped up again, kicked the table, and said, 'Damn it, damn it, you can't keep them out of anything.'

* * *

Anselm walked back and forth for exercise. He passed his favourite tree, the flowering pear. He had stood for a quarter of an hour in front of it the night before, astonished at how its pale petals held the light so that he was able to see the whole tree blooming in the darkness.

In the daytime the tree seemed smaller than it had at night. He wondered why that should be. Maybe it had appeared large in isolation and because of being surrounded by black: a trick of the light and of the eye perceiving it. Or maybe the night showed the truth and the daytime tree was deceptively small.

He dropped all his duties and lived a life of ease. Most of the brothers felt that he had a certain amount of justification for it, though not necessarily because he had been touched by God. Everyone knew now that he had turned or been turned into a woman, and that was enough to excuse a lot. That in itself was a breach of discipline. It was breaking the rules like nobody's business.

A few people agreed with Brother Adrian and sat with him for hours at a stretch, discussing just what evil, unnatural, or evilly unnatural, or unnaturally evil cause could be behind the whole thing. But most of the young ones were on

Anselm's side. And in his own wing of the building he became a focal point for afternoon meetings. He had a little club of admirers. They were zealously noted by Adrian and his followers, who reported the members to Frederick. But when Frederick suggested stamping out the coterie, Francis persuaded him that that would just make everything worse. They were to wait.

'There's a right time for everything, you know,' Frederick said. 'Remember the Bible. Sometimes it's a mistake to wait.'

'Not this time,' Francis told him. 'And that isn't what that passage is about, anyway. Calm down, Frederick.'

Anselm's friends brought him quantities of pillows, many of them silk and satin, to help support his back. He lay reclined on them like an oriental princess, smiling sweetly at the other brothers as they confided their troubles to him.

They drank coffee or tea or wine. Sometimes they'd flirt with him. Brother Elmo was especially obstreperous. You could still see the pierce-mark where he'd worn the earring in his left ear; he'd received the call, so he said, on a trip. 'A trip to where?' Brother William had asked. 'A trip to outer space, man. A trip on speed. Get in focus, Billy.'

Elmo was delighted with Anselm's transfiguration. It proved, he claimed, that he'd been right all along: anything could happen in life, and everything did, only most people were so unaware, so lacking in powers of observation, that they didn't notice. He stared possessively at Anselm and asked, 'So when are you going to let us have some fun with you, babe? It better be soon, before you get too big.'

'Don't be naughty,' Anselm said. He made a motion of hitting at Elmo with a small peacock-feather fan that had come wrapped up with one of the pillows.

'Come on, Anselm. We're your friends, aren't we? Who else are you going to play around with if it isn't your friends?'

'It's not a joke.'

'At least let us see your tits.'

Anselm fanned himself lazily.

'We'll bring you some extra food. You're eating for two now, remember.'

'I do have these terrible strong desires for certain tastes: dill pickles, cheesecake, raspberry ice cream, walnut and pecan mousse, smoked mackerel and watermelons.'

'We'll get them for you.'

'Promise?'

All the brothers nodded vehemently. Anselm undid his robe and exposed the full, cup-shaped breasts of which he was now immensely proud. There was a silence until he started to pull the robe together again.

'Wait,' Dominic said, and William begged, 'Not yet. I haven't finished looking.'

'Crazy, man,' Elmo said.

'Weird,' said Dominic.

'Cute. They look just like a girl.'

'Weird.'

'Can I touch one of them, Anselm?'

'Certainly not.'

'Why not? I just want to feel.'

'That's all meant for the baby, you know.'

'How did you work it?' William asked. 'How did you get them to grow? Did you wake up in the morning and find them like that?'

'No, it happened gradually. They got a little bigger every day.'

'Did it hurt?'

'Not hurt, exactly. Everything felt very tender and sore all over my chest. And so forth.' He snapped up the front of his robe again.

Brother James, at the back of the group, said he thought he had an explanation. 'Maybe –' he said, 'it's got something to do with radioactive fall-out from the atom bombs.'

'Or Mount St Helen's,' Dominic added.

'It was the angel,' Anselm said. 'I told them in the first place. It was Gabriel.'

* * *

109

'They're sitting around drinking wine in there,' Frederick said. 'Next thing you know, there'll be luxury and vicious- ness all over the place. Everybody knows about the stimulat- ing properties of alcohol.'

'We should,' Francis said. 'We make a living out of it. They're just talking.'

'It makes me jumpy.'

'How can you stop them being interested? It's an abso- lutely extraordinary thing.'

'It's unnatural.'

'It's what happened to Our Blessed Lady.'

'I don't want to get into that argument. Anyway, when it happened to Mary, it wasn't a sin. It was pure. This is terrible.'

'You've been listening to Brother Adrian.'

'He talks a lot of sense sometimes, in spite of being a little over-emphatic.'

'Crass. He's a crass man, and frightened. And now he's infected you. Did you drink up all the whisky? That's right, he always has that effect on you.'

'Unnatural,' Frederick insisted.

'How can it be unnatural if it's happened?'

'It shouldn't have happened.'

'What do you call conception through the ear-hole? That's supposed to be the way the Holy Ghost got in, isn't it?'

'We have to regard these events in a philosophic light, as representing symbolic manifestations of spiritual truths.'

'What?'

'And Brother Anselm just isn't in that league. Also, the whole thing is against the teachings of Mother Church.'

'Nonsense. A miracle is a miracle is a miracle.'

'Is that what you really think this is?'

'I don't know what it is. Truly.'

'Brother Duncan says he thinks Anselm was androg . . . an andr . . . whatever the word is.'

'Hermaphrodite?'

'And he lived all one way for years, even though the other

110

half was there all the time, lurking under the surface, just waiting to show itself – which it finally did, all at once.'

'Complete with child?'

'No. That came later. First of all he hid it and had carnal relations with somebody in here, and when he found out he was pregnant, then he came to you.'

'Neat.'

'The whole rigmarole is having a profoundly unsettling effect on the order.'

'Especially on you.'

'On me too, of course. I don't deny it. But look at Adrian. And in the other direction – what about Marcus?'

Brother Marcus had become a regular visitor to Anselm's room. He had been so completely won over that it was now his greatest pride to be responsible for making Anselm look as attractive as possible. He delighted in finding new arrangements in which to set Anselm's luxuriant dark hair, which was growing so quickly that it was already down to his shoulders. 'Let's put it up today,' Marcus would suggest, or, 'How about side-swept for a change?' He came every morning and evening, his sausagelike fingers deft among the glossy masses of hair. He had managed to acquire a set of pins and ornaments for keeping the hair in place and twining it into piled-up shapes. And while he worked, a light of happiness shone from his face. He had changed. He'd always looked as strong and coarse as a picture of a Victorian butcher, but now he displayed moods of elephantinely delicate playfulness and good humour.

'God Almighty,' Brother Adrian said under his breath as Anselm moved up to the table with his slow, billowing gait and his elaborately perched hair-do, 'it's like sitting down to dinner with the Whore of Babylon.'

'You should be so lucky,' Brother Robert told him. 'What I hear is: he doesn't sell it and he doesn't give it away for free. Admiration from afar is his line.'

'Maybe he's saving himself for another bout with the supernatural.'

111

'If it's true,' Brother James said, 'no amount of repentance is going to make up for the way you're talking about him now.'

'It isn't true,' Adrian told him. 'And it's a blasphemy even to think it might be.'

*   *   *

Before Frederick's era, the monastery had been run by Father Clement. He had been a rather absent-minded, scholarly person, until Vatican Two. And then he threw over the traces with a vengeance. As Frederick had said at the time, no one could have suspected such an intense urge towards chaos in the man. All at once Father Clement espoused every cause and crackpot movement that had been hitting the headlines for the past three decades while he'd been supposed to be tilling the vineyards and praising the Lord. He went from Flower Power to Hard Rock in three weeks. He became interested in Scientology. And he allowed anybody in: Hell's Angels, ballet dancers, health food freaks and gigolos.

That was the trouble with tolerance: you could get too much of it. Too much – and people stampeded over you. The time came when Father Clement welcomed a set of what were to anyone else's eyes ordinary winos so far gone in the abuse of alcohol that they were already brain-damaged. There was a scandal. The papers got hold of it. It was deplorable; atrocious. Father Clement was now, so everyone believed, in Hawaii, teaching Shakespeare to the Japanese. And the monastery was still awaiting a replacement, although in the meantime Brother Frederick was in command. It meant a great deal to Frederick that his interregnum should be peaceable and well-ordered. A promotion to the top was more than merely possible.

He had thought that he'd begin by weeding out the more sinister or cranky newcomers, but by the time he took over, the men were leaving so quickly they were practically tripping over each other trying to get to the door. They were like the rats leaving a sinking ship. And then, miraculously, the new influx arrived, even younger: a fresh generation of believers; however, their belief wasn't of the old quality, their education up to the same level. Some of them had had hardly any religious instruction at all. 'Beggars can't be choosers,' Brother Robert had said over his wine one evening. 'God', Frederick had answered grandly, 'does not need to beg.' Robert had given him a pitying look and shaken his head, and almost immediately been proven right: a bad flu rampaged through the order, turning the place into a geriatric ward. The old monks began to die off. Those who didn't die had to be cleaned, fed and manoeuvred on to bedpans. Frederick realized that he wasn't going to be able to kick many young men out. The solution would be to keep them there and change them into better monks. And, all in all, having had inferior material to work with, he hadn't done too badly. He was proud of his record.

Sometimes he thought about the ones his own age who had left – who had voluntarily jettisoned the calling to which they had been dedicated, reneged on their vocations. He thought of them as deserters or, at times, escapees. They thought of him, too. A lot of them regularly sent postcards and letters back from the outside. When he was feeling particularly glum and grouchy, he'd remember the messages:

> *I never knew what living was like till I left the order.*
> *What are you trying to prove?*
> *Come on in, the water's fine.*
> *Freddie, you're a jerk to stay.*

Often the more strait-laced they had been, the more fatuous their greetings were. The Classicists had gone, to become pragmatists. The Romantics stayed.

Brother Francis used to say that there was no need to keep anyone who didn't have faith. As far as the vineyards went, they could hire workers. The order was dedicated to God – there was no necessity, and should be none, to accept anyone below standard. But Robert told him, 'We just cannot afford to turn down men who come to us for our novelty-value. We have to assume that there's a genuine desire underlying the frivolous impulse.' And it was true that now you could see he'd been as acute about that as about the grapes. They'd had many vintage years for wine lately; not so many for men. They needed the numbers.

Most of Anselm's admirers were entirely untutored; they'd had no religious training in childhood. Many of them had come to their faith, as he had, under the pressure of some dramatic event or crisis. Elmo, who had served with the Oakland Fire Department, had preserved the lives of people who later tried to murder each other; and he had failed to rescue the innocent. He'd had a breakdown after a particularly ferocious tenement conflagration in which the only member of a large and quarrelsome family that he hadn't been able to save was the baby: it lay at the top of the house, its lungs scorched by smoke, while the demented relatives down below shrieked with frustration and beat him nearly to death, calling him a son of a bitch and a bastard. He had been furious, ashamed, and found that whenever he remembered the helpless baby up at the top of the fiery house, he wanted to cry. It took him six months to work out his thoughts and feelings. In the end, it came down to a simple formula: if there was nothing, he couldn't stand it; but if there was something, then in some way – even though no one knew exactly how – the baby was all right.

William's conversion had come through someone else: his young wife, who had fallen from an open stairway on a pier and hit one of the boats near their own. She had injured her spine so badly that at first the doctors thought she'd die in a few hours. It took her weeks, and during that time she was in agony. William had stayed with her right up to the end, when she suddenly received a revelation of God and said that the pain had vanished completely. She was dying then; they had a few final days together and William caught her belief as if it had been a germ in the hospital. But he didn't want to be cured of it afterwards. He was happy with the monastic life – that is, he was happy until the strange business about Anselm took over.

Dominic's was another case of hospitalization, though he had been the chief actor in the drama: he had been struck by lightning, thrown forty feet into a neighbouring field, and was in the hospital for four weeks recovering. Then he was at home for three months, just thinking about it. Twelve cows in the same field had been killed by the bolt. He had an idea that he'd been given a warning of some kind because his life wasn't the model of righteousness it was designed to be. A cow was a very big animal; twelve of them had died, yet he had been spared. That seemed to be a sign. He made preparations to try to save his soul.

James was different. He'd gone to Italy on a holiday after college. 'I was such a hick,' he said. 'I didn't know anything. Some friends asked me to the opera, and that's how it began. I stayed longer than I'd intended to. Then another friend took me to see the mosaics in Ravenna. And that's how I became a Christian. I had no idea of the way of life. That all came later. I'm probably the only example you'll ever meet of the redemptive power of art. Nature, and human nature, is so much more impressive.'

'And how about you, Anselm?' the brothers asked.

Anselm had started out in the order by keeping the books, as he had done in the world outside. He had entered just in time to take over from a Brother Timothy, who died, as everyone had expected, the next day. In view of the fact that the auditing was just about to come up, Anselm's arrival was seen as providential.

He had been trained as an accountant, had jobs in various small firms and then begun to work in large corporations, finally settling in a well-paid and interesting job at a bank. He was ready to branch out in his career and aim for the heights, when one day he saw a newsreel about surfboarding. The next morning he quit work and went down to the beach.

He had decided to become an expert. Only the experts could ride the big waves out in the islands: the ones like the one in the movie, which had shown a huge wall of green glass quivering forward, and – tracing a thin white line across the middle of it – a tiny dot: the surfer. He wanted to be good enough to go through the really dangerous waves – the ones that curled over on themselves, forming a tube, so that you could ride down the centre as if going through a tunnel; but, because your feet would be lashed to the board in case it bounced up, threw you, and came back to hit you on the head at a hundred miles an hour, you'd be in danger of losing your foot: if a sharp piece of coral caught you as you were going by, that was it – the foot would be sliced off. At least that would be better, the other surfers told him, than getting killed by your board.

He got night work in factories and as a watchman in warehouses. He finally found a job in a vast complex of storage buildings where he worked with two men who agreed with him to spell each other so that two of them could always get six hours' unbroken sleep every night. And then he found the right day, when all the waves were perfect. And the right wave – just like the one in the newsreel – which he knew would never end; he'd be able to ride it for ever all around the world from ocean to ocean.

And then all at once, unexpectedly, he was in the water. Something had slammed him hard on his head, shoulders and back and he was under the surface, not knowing which way was up. He must have taken a breath instinctively and saved his life that way. But soon he started to thrash around in terror. He needed air. He fought wildly – luckily without success, since the water itself buoyed him to the surface against his efforts. He was saved. And from those moments of remembered fear, his wish for a faith was born. Looking back, he figured out that – unlikely as it seemed – he must have been struck by some kind of fish jumping from the sea; a board or any other hard object would have broken every bone in his body. But the agent of the accident was a minor question. The truly puzzling mystery was his survival.

He simply couldn't understand how he had escaped death if something else hadn't been helping him. What could it have been? What was more powerful than a great force of nature like the sea?

'That was how it started,' he said. 'I tried to think it out. But now I know thought is useless when it comes to the important things.'

*   *   *

The front of Anselm's robe was studded and stuck with the trinkets and tokens he'd been given by other monks. Some of the gifts looked like votary offerings. He never asked where they came from. For years the cells and cloisters of the monastery had been bare of ornament; now from nowhere shiny buttons and pins appeared, so that they could be presented to Anselm.

'The creature is positively bedizened,' Brother Adrian snarled. 'Decorated like a Christmas tree.' He got drunk for two days and couldn't be roused.

'You see', Frederick told Francis, 'the effect it's having.'

'Just on Adrian. He was nearly this bad over the legal rights on the new vineyard eight years ago. Remember? That's the way he is. He wouldn't be tolerated for a minute in the outside world.'

'Don't kid yourself – he'd be one of the ones running it. And in his clearer moments, he's actually extremely capable.'

'But not likeable. Even talent has its limits.'

Frederick heaved an enormous sigh. He threw up his hands to heaven and for a few seconds scrabbled at the air before sighing again and returning to normal. 'I got three postcards today,' he said. 'Brother Aloysius has become a Buddhist. He says he doesn't hold anything against us.'

'That's nice of him.'

'Ungrateful old swine. I hope they have as much trouble with him as we did.'

They turned to the right by the chapel and saw Anselm in the distance.

'What do you think?' Francis said.

117

'Oh, it's a mess. Just the kind of slipshod entanglement a boy like Anselm would be apt to get himself into.'

'Not a miracle?'

'Are there such things?'

'You know very well there are. But maybe you have to wait for somebody else to tell you that's what they are.'

'Your nasty moments are always so refreshing, Francis. One doesn't expect them.'

'I put it badly. What I meant was that it's like seeing a new movie or a new play. Some people say it's all right, one or two that it's wonderful, and a lot say it's worthless. Or the other way around. In time, everyone knows what to think. When something is completely new, it's got to be fitted into its place. It has to be assimilated. And every age has its miracles.'

* * *

Anselm looked through the papers. He came across a story about a Chinese boy who could read through his ears instead of his eyes; they'd blindfold him, hold a book up to his right ear, and let him read it. (The left ear appeared to be illiterate.)

He turned to a page near the back. A column next to the gardening news reported the uncanny ability of a five-year-old girl to turn tennis balls inside-out by the power of thought. And in the same issue there was a short item that told of a man who had died from just drinking water. He'd drunk thirty-five pints. According to friends of his, he'd said that he was 'trying to clean out his system'.

He started to order books from the public library. He got them through Brother Duncan, whose attitude towards him was becoming irritatingly proprietorial. The books were all about babies and the habits that could be discerned in them as soon as they were born. The romping movements, Anselm read, were for exercise; the grabbing and clinging instinct apparently went way back to the time when the human young would have to be able to get a grip on the mother's fur.

'Fur?' Elmo said. 'Have you been holding out on us? We thought you only had the usual accessories.'

'Shh,' Anselm told him. He continued to read from the book. The brothers were fascinated. Everyone wanted to help bring up the baby.

Eventually they talked about what sort of a child it would be, why it had been 'sent', and how they should educate it. Or perhaps it would be enough just to love it.

Other monks, at the far side of the cloister, also talked. Two of them on the way to Matins hurried across the courtyard together. One said, 'She came among us in a disguised form. That's why we didn't recognize her.' The other said, 'No, it's just the reverse. He's in a disguised form now.' It was like a quarrel about whether a dog was white with black spots or black with white spots. And, in any case, they weren't supposed to be discussing it.

* * *

Deep in thought, Anselm strolled along the pillared porches. In the distance he could see William standing still and looking intently, forlornly, at him.

Anselm moved closer. William began to edge nearer. He was in love with Anselm. He had picked a blossoming branch as an emblem of his love and wanted to offer it, but didn't quite dare.

Anselm rocked gracefully towards him, the swell of his skirt bearing him forward as if by sail or by balloon. He reached the spot where William stood transfixed by the sight of him. Anselm gave him a soft glance; the long lashes over his dark eyes were longer than ever. 'Hello, William,' he said.

'I wanted to give you this,' William told him. He held out the branch.

Anselm recognized the flowers as part of his favourite tree. He blinked languidly.

'For the baby,' William whispered.

Anselm took the branch. 'Thank you, William,' he said. 'How sweet of you.'

William dropped to his knees. He caught the edge of Anselm's robe in his hands and buried his face in it.

119

Anselm bent down slowly, touched William's head as if in blessing, and passed on.

William remained on his knees and began to pray.

* * *

'You've seen how Brother William is taking it?' Adrian demanded.

'A simple heart,' Frederick said.

'Rife for corruption.'

'Ripe.'

'This place could become a hotbed of debauchery over-night.'

'Really, Adrian, I think that's overstating the case.'

'All I want to know is what you're going to do about it.'

'You leave that to me.'

'No, Frederick. We've all waited long enough. If I don't see some action, I'm reporting it.'

'Be careful, Adrian. If you go too far, you'll be confined to quarters. I don't want any heroics out of you.'

'Me?' Brother Adrian cried. His tone was one of wounded innocence, his face nearly purple. Frederick knew that this mood of his was even harder to deal with than his rages.

* * *

Anselm waited for Francis outside the chapel until an older monk, Brother Theodore, had left. Then he came forward.

'Francis, may I ask you a question?'

'Certainly.' He hadn't heard Anselm's approach and was startled by the way he looked – so obviously pregnant, so like a young woman of the ancient world as it was pictured by the great Renaissance painters; and so pretty.

'This isn't a confession,' Anselm said.

'That's all right. Sit down.'

They sat in the pews, Anselm sliding in sideways and near a corner, to rest his back. 'What I want to know,' he said, 'is if you think that after the birth I should continue to lead a single life.'

'I hadn't thought that far, as a matter of fact.'

'Because there's somebody who loves me. And I feel that we'd be very well matched and everything. And a child needs a father.'

'Yes,' Francis said. 'But supposing – I mean, perhaps it would end up having two of them. It might be possible that after the birth, you'd go back to the way you were.'

'It might. Anything could happen. In that case, I'd have to find a mother for my child instead, wouldn't I?'

'Not necessarily. You could raise it alone. After the first few weeks, it's the father that's important: a figure of authority. A loving authority.'

'That doesn't matter. Authority is what you are or where you stand, not whether you're male or female. It's politically determined.'

'Authorities are male.'

'Only because things are organized like that.'

'But if you're trying to come to a decision, that makes a difference, doesn't it?'

'I guess. And I'd become so fond of this person.'

'Brother William?'

'Sweet William. Before the Annunciation, I used to think he was a bit of an oaf. Now he seems so nice – true-hearted and full of life.'

'If you reverted to your former state, you might return to your first opinion of him. It might go with the alteration. So maybe you'd better wait.'

Anselm ran a hand through his hair, rumpling the sleekly regimented locks. 'I'd thought all the problems were solved,' he said, 'everything taken care of.'

'It's causing a lot of complications around you, you know.'

'Oh, that. That's just people's attitudes.'

'I worry about it.'

'Good. You can worry about it for me. I'm not going to.'

'Anselm, I do worry. Not everyone is kind. And it isn't everyone who can take the detached view.'

121

'Well, do you have an answer?'

'You haven't been to Mass in a very great while.'

'No.'

'It's for your sake, not mine or ours.'

'Don't let it bother you, Francis. I'm in God's hands.'

'We're all in God's hands. I just thought – well, I don't know. Your prayers are important, too. It isn't enough just to exist and not take part.'

'But every minute I live is given to God. He sent his angel. He – '

'The Mass, Anselm.'

'For me, that's secondhand now.'

'That's a very arrogant and wrong-headed thing to say.'

'Why? It's true.'

'Oh dear,' Brother Francis said.

* * *

'I don't want any X-rays.'

Brother Duncan said, 'It isn't an X-ray. It's a scan for finding out if the baby's going to be a girl or a boy.'

'Scan – what does that mean?'

'It's – '

'You can hear the heartbeat. Isn't that all right? And you can feel it kicking now. We'll find out what sex it is when it's born.'

'It would be nice to know now.'

'Nice for who?'

'Aren't you curious?'

'Doctor, I want you to promise me something. This child has got to be born alive and well, whether it's normal or not.'

'Who says it isn't going to be normal?'

'I want you to promise. The decision is not yours. Do you understand?'

'I've taken the Hippocratic oath, Anselm.'

'And we all know how much that's worth.'

'Who's been filling your mind with these fears?'

122

'They come naturally. It's an anxious time. Look at all my badges and buttons. I'm superstitious about everything now. I've got to be able to trust you. I know you don't believe what happened, but I've got to have your help.'

'I definitely believe you changed sex. There's no doubt about that.'

'I'm asking you as a doctor, and also as a Christian. The temptation is going to be great. They're leaning on you, aren't they?'

'There's a certain amount of pressure, of course. That's my problem. I can handle it.'

'Since I've been pregnant, I've begun to understand a lot of things about doctors and women – telling them what to do, regulating them, applying a system. I used to think there were so many more male doctors than female ones just because it's such a highly paid job, but now I'm not sure. Now I'm coming to believe it's all to do with power – that men look at all other creatures as things on which to practice their power, that they think freedom means being able to carry out that practice; and they don't like it if anyone is really free just to be the way they are.'

'Anselm, you're going to find that you're increasingly prey to all kinds of fears, but – believe me, they have no foundation. I'm a doctor; I know.'

'You may be a doctor, Duncan, but compared to me, you're an ignoramus.'

'Thanks a bunch.'

'My knowledge comes directly from God.'

'So you've said.'

'Where do you think this child came from?'

'I'm not asking that question. I'm interested in facts as they are.'

'But they're so changeable. Facts can change in an instant. That's what happened to me. It's like peacetime and wartime, like happiness and sorrow. You never know when the change is going to come.'

'But not like male and female.'

123

'How do you know?'

'Do you think you're the only person this so-called visitation ever happened to? Except the first instance, I mean.'

'I've wondered about that, too. All I can say is that if there were others, they kept quiet about it. Or it was hushed up. Or no one believed it. That would be the most likely explanation. Not many people here believe me, either.'

'You don't think you're the only one?'

'I do. But that may only be because everything that happens to people seems to be special to them. It seems unique.'

'I've never heard or read of anything like it. The occasional hysterical woman, yes – nothing like this.'

'That's the trouble. Right from the start it was medically exciting. You still think it's the prize-winning case-history. But they're giving you orders about me, aren't they?'

'Nobody wants anything but your own good, Anselm.'

'And if they didn't, what could I do about it? It's giving me the creeps. Look at the way I am. How could I defend myself? They're all running themselves in circles about scandal and reputation and theology. This matters more. If you're any kind of a doctor, there must have been a time when you thought so too.'

'I wanted to become a doctor,' Duncan said, 'because I wanted to know about the human soul, life and death, where people went to when they died, why they were the way they were. I studied in the laboratories, in mortuaries. I had parts of people on the table in front of me like pieces of a Sunday chicken. We had all kinds of things – insides – to look at. When I was a student, I had a collection of innards in jars. A whole shelf full. I even had a foetus in a bottle. I studied it. I also used to wonder about it a lot – whether it was a miscarriage, or whether the mother wanted to get rid of it; a lot of them do, you know. A lot of them wouldn't give you two cents for the Hippocratic oath. It seemed to me at that time: even more important than the question of where we

124

went, was the question of where we came from. The embryo I
owned was a person. They were all, all the pieces in jars. . . .
Then I got to thinking about how the whole of that side of life
was entrusted to women. And that was where my understanding broke down. They're so patently unworthy. Strange as
your case is, Anselm, the one thing about it that makes sense
to me is that, if it's true, it should have been a man who was
chosen this time. If that's what happened.'

'That's what happened. But that isn't the part I think is
important. I'm the same. I'm the same person now that I was
then. I've got a different body, that's all. Do you think we're
what our bodies are?'

'We live inside them. We inhabit them. We're influenced
by them, very. The state of a person's health can change his
personality.'

'It can't change him into something he had no capacity for
from the beginning. Or can it?'

'You think you were a woman all along?'

'I think I was chosen, and because the female body is the
one made for carrying and feeding children, I was given that.
Do you think I'm going to change back afterwards?'

'What?'

'As soon as I stop breast-feeding, do you think I'll go back
to being a man?'

'Oh my God, Anselm.'

'It's like a joke, isn't it?'

'It simply never occurred to me.'

'I hadn't thought that far myself. I was just happy. But now
I'm beginning to get a little anxious. I don't want anything to
go wrong.'

'Nothing will go wrong. Relax. You're very healthy.'

Anselm stood up. It took him several movements now. He
felt as ungainly as a camel getting to its feet.

He went for a walk in the courtyard and then down past
the potato gardens. He stopped a few times to think. He
leaned against one of the stone walls in the garden and partly
closed his eyes. He remembered the way it had been at the

beginning: Gabriel alighting on the green square of grass. Once again, like warmth from a flame or a breath·from the air, the remembered touch ran tickling over his skin.

He knew that the central event was all right and assured. His worries were all about the peripheral effects. Whether man or woman, he was living in the world as it was at a particular time. And in most parts of the country, despite the revolution in morals, changed attitudes towards sexual freedom, the high incidence of divorce and the promulgation of certain doctrines by the women's movements – still, in general, illegitimacy was disapproved of. Because he was single, things were going to be made difficult for him. And if he remained single, they'd be made difficult for the child too. There were hundreds of ways in which a child could be hurt, shocked, shamed or cruelly teased by other children at school. Schools were full of quarrels and fights and name-calling.

On his way back to his cell he went near the chapel, where the brothers were singing Compline. The baby began to move boisterously. Whenever there was music, it kicked hard. Anselm thought maybe it picked up the vibrations and was trying to dance.

He passed by, going to the right and down the hallway that led to his corridor. A burst of laughter came from behind one of the closed doors; shouted opinions followed. There seemed to be at least three, perhaps four voices. Anselm heard himself named and turned back.

'What I think – ' one of the voices said.

Another one interrupted: 'She's asking for it.'

'Miracle, my arse.' The voice could have been the first man again, or a different one. Through the closed door it was hard to tell. One of them said something in a low murmur that Anselm didn't catch. The others cackled like witches. He could guess, from the remark that had gone before, what kind of comment it had been. After that, there was a loud crash and a despairing cry: 'Jesus fucking Christ, you've done it again.'

'Not so loud.'

'Second one you've broken.'

'Shut up.'

'Let's have some more blood of the lamb, Brother Eustace.'

'Let's go pay Sister Anselm a call.'

'One more drink.'

'I don't want to get mixed up in anything like that. He's got a lot of friends now.'

'I wouldn't give a plug nickel for his friends. My friends are bigger than anybody's friends.'

'I don't give a damn. I don't give . . . I don't give a whatever, not about anything.'

'It might be true.'

'Oh, come on.'

'I'm not saying it is, but you just tell me how you can explain it.'

'It's a rip-off, of course.'

'What kind of a rip-off can do that?'

'What I think is, we shouldn't take it for granted.'

'Take what for granted? What are you talking about now?'

'Anything, anything. You should never take nothing for granted. Eyesight, now – a wonderful thing, a marvel. It can be lost in a second. That's true, you know. I have a brother-in-law; but never mind. What I'm saying is, you shouldn't count on it. Course, in the end we lose everything: sight, hearing, so on.'

'Jesus, don't get so gloomy. You're spoiling the fun. How could we lose everything?'

'Getting old.'

'That isn't so bad. I know a lot of pretty happy old people. Well, not a lot. Some.'

'And then we die.'

A different voice said, 'But we live again in Christ.'

'Well,' the first man answered, 'it's a nice thought.'

Anselm felt dizzy. He made his way to his room, lay down on the bed and closed his eyes. He thought he'd like to pray lying down, since it was so uncomfortable getting on to his knees and having to bend forward.

He put his hands together. 'Holy Mary,' he began, and stopped. He couldn't think of anything more to say.

Surely, he thought, William would understand. If he remained the way he was, a woman, they could stay together as a family. And if he changed back, they could split up, or even keep on going like that, too.

He didn't join the others for supper. Dominic brought him a bowl of soup, some bread and butter and an apple.

'Aren't you feeling well, Anselm?' he asked.

'Sure. I'm all right. Just tired.'

'You take care of yourself. We've all got bets riding on you.'

'What's the verdict?'

'Oh, everybody thinks it's going to be a boy. If it's a girl, about three people are going to clean up. They'd be millionaires. Everybody else would be out in the cold. You want a boy too, of course, don't you?'

'Naturally. That's the way it's supposed to be.' He drank his soup and felt better. Brother Ignatius and Brother Sebastian in the kitchen were working overtime now, making sure that nothing sat too heavily on his stomach.

He started to feel still better late in the night when he thought about the birth. He was afraid of the pain but he was certain that the event was going to be of such cataclysmic importance and excitement that the pain would have to become secondary. And it would all be worth it, anyway. Now that he could feel the baby pushing and bumping, he was beginning to know it. It kept him company. He talked to it. He told it stories – things he made up, as well as the more traditional fairytales he remembered from his own childhood.

Once upon a time, he said to himself, *there were three bears: a mamma bear, a pappa bear and a baby bear.* There was a king who had three daughters, a woodcutter with three sons. *Once upon a time there were three little pigs and they all lived in the forest, where there was a big, bad wolf.* Everything went in threes and everything was told as if it had happened only that week, or it could just as easily have been centuries ago. *Once upon a time*, he thought, *there was the Father, the Son and the Holy Ghost.*

* * *

'Brother Adrian', Francis said, 'is in trouble. I think he's going out of his mind, Frederick.'

'No more than usual. And he's always got emotional troubles. You know Adrian – that's the way he is. He runs on it: it's like a fuel. Francis, I want to ask you to help me with something.'

'I don't know how much good advice I've got left for today.'

'I don't need advice. What I'm going to need is your vote. I want to get William transferred.'

'That would be hard on Anselm, just as his time is drawing so near.'

'Francis, they're planning to get married.'

'Not yet. I think they're going to wait till after the birth. To find out if Anselm reverts.'

'Judas Priest, there's no end to the ramifications. This whole thing has degenerated into a farce. It's preposterous.'

'It's a mystery, Frederick. That's what it was from the beginning, and that's never changed. The rest is what we make out of it.'

'No.'

'We interpret and we explain. But the central fact is the only truth, and it's inexplicable.'

'It was a sign and I failed to act on it. I didn't even see it till the business about William. Francis, I've missed the boat – I should have gone to a higher authority right at the beginning, and I didn't. Now it's too late. I didn't recognize this as the great trial of my life – of all our lives. No, I don't believe it's a miracle, damn it. But I do believe it's here to test us. And I've been found wanting.'

'Don't be silly.'

'In my own eyes, first of all. But what are the others going to say?'

'They wouldn't have acted any differently.'

'Who knows? You never know these things till they happen. You say to yourself, "If. If." But that's no guide. Brother William has got to go.'

'If we sent Brother Adrian away instead –'

'He's only an outside irritation. Brother William is about to become intimately involved.'

'Do you dislike Anselm?'

'Of course not. I resent the confusion he's caused, that's all. He causes it, I have to deal with it. If you can't help me with William, it's Anselm who'll have to go. Either way, they've got to be kept apart.'

'I just don't see why.'

Frederick settled himself deeply into his chair. There were three ways he could appeal to Francis's fears, hopes and sense of right. He prepared to use them all in the order of their power to tempt and persuade. He said, 'Very well. We'll go through it again till you do.'

* * *

'That's right,' Brother James told Anselm. 'He wasn't at supper and he wasn't at breakfast. They drove him away in the early evening.'

Elmo and Dominic corroborated the story. Elmo said he'd heard from a Brother Anthony that the car had left from the kitchen entrance. Brother Ignatius had seen it.

Anselm held tightly to the crumpled paper he'd been handed by Marcus when he'd come to do his hair that morning. The note was from William, who said that he was being moved to another place, that he would remain true and never forget him, that Anselm and the baby would be in his thoughts and prayers, and that William loved him.

'It was Adrian,' Elmo declared.

Anselm said, 'It was Frederick.'

'Brother Adrian's been bucking all month to get at least one of us out. But don't worry. You've still got friends.'

'Adrian wouldn't have the authority. Somebody had to

130

take the responsibility for this. The only one it could have been is the man at the top.'

'It's incredible how everything always ends up political,' Dominic said.

'It's because the structure is political,' Elmo told him. 'Anything extra you put in it is going to assume that shape.'

'He won't see me,' Anselm said. 'I've asked for an appointment and he won't give me one. I can only talk to Francis.'

'Are you coming to eat?' James asked.

'I'm banned. I'm lucky I haven't been confined to my room.'

'We'll do something about it,' James said. 'This is beyond the limit.'

Anselm nodded feebly. He held the letter to his heart and turned his head away.

*   *   *

When he woke, Brother Sebastian was bringing in a cup of soup and some crackers. 'They're having a big fight,' he whispered. As soon as he'd put down the tray, he started to hop with impatience, gesturing towards the door. 'Brother Eustace and Adrian against the others. When I left, they were all screaming like monkeys. I'll be back later, Anselm. I want to see what happens.'

Anselm waved his hand graciously. He started on the soup and flipped through a new magazine that had arrived in the morning mail. On the cover was a picture of a really darling baby, just the kind he wanted.

*   *   *

In the dining-room no single voice could be heard above the total uproar. All the brothers were yelling and pelting each other with food. A few of them were throwing bowls and bottles, too. Francis was socked hard in the side of the head while trying to make peace between one man holding a broken glass and another one brandishing a knife. He lost his

131

hearing for a moment and had to sit down. He put his hands over his ears and let the tumult rage around him. Frederick, who had played right half-back at the seminary, fought his way to the door. He punched and jabbed a great many brothers on his way out and left the room feeling satisfied and invigorated.

*   *   *

Anselm read through the letters to the editor in his magazine. He liked finding out about how new mothers felt and what problems they had to contend with.

The first letter was from a woman who wanted to know how she could overcome her fear that friends who came to the house were going to pass on their microbes and bacteria to her baby. The editor advised her to relax and stop worrying. Anselm thought she had a point: these things were, after all, invisible. The second writer asked why sanitary towels weren't state-subsidized, as she was finding them increasingly expensive and it wasn't her fault that she had to have them – all women of child-bearing age needed them; they couldn't help it. The editor said that as a matter of fact, in poorer countries where people weren't so well-nourished, the women didn't wear any special clothing against menstruation and only ever saw a couple of drops of blood in a month; so, if you were healthy enough to menstruate heavily, that probably meant you were rich enough to afford the kotex and tampax.

The third, and last, letter was from a woman who claimed that according to her experience, unmarried mothers in the hospital she'd been in were treated with a coldness, hostility and neglect that could be dangerous for the child and certainly contributed to the mother's sense of loneliness and inferiority. Many of the nurses, she said, came from strongly religious backgrounds, and she thought it was a shame that people who were supposed to believe in peace and love-thy-neighbour should be so unfeeling, snobbish and narrow-minded.

Of course, Anselm thought; it would be true. No matter what the woman herself thought, the doctors and nurses

132

would regard the pregnancy as an unfortunate, unplanned and unwanted accident, maybe even thinking they would be doing the mother a favour to let the child die.

He slapped the pages of the magazine together and threw it aside. He had always imagined that women enjoyed a special kind of freedom because nothing was ever going to be expected of them, but now he saw that they were just as trapped as men. He had to find a husband, and as soon as possible. It didn't matter now whether it was someone he was genuinely fond of, like William, or a man he didn't care about at all. Anybody would do, and for the baby's sake any deception would be justified. He shouldn't have second thoughts about explaining anything, or mentioning possible future transformations. Whatever the nurses were like in the hospital Duncan had chosen, he was certain their prejudices would be the same as those of other nurses. And even before he got that far, there was his life in the monastery to consider. Brother Adrian had forced Frederick to remove William: there was no telling what might happen next.

Well, he thought, he was going to have to start being like other people – to set things up and make them come true, to hustle and manipulate. He'd have to try to get rid of his enemies. If he were alone, he wouldn't care; but for the baby's sake, he had to.

Frederick could hurt him officially. But Adrian was more dangerous: violent and unpredictable. And he made Frederick nervous enough to feel compelled to act.

Anselm got up and went for a walk through the cloisters. He heard a commotion coming from the dining-halls. The monks sounded like howling spectators at a football game. He kept going, down corridors and across courtyards.

He came to his favourite tree. It was a different shape because it was in leaf now. It seemed also to look older. First it was in bud, then all blossom, then covered in leaves, then came the fruit. And next year, all over again; like the stages of a woman's life.

*   *   *

Soon after lunch Brother Adrian went berserk and had to be taken away in a straitjacket. Before the jacket, they had used a rope.

Anselm had seen him rushing from the direction of the dining-rooms and coming towards him very fast, oblivious to everything around him until all at once he realized that Anselm was only a few yards away. He stopped dead, his pudgy, engorged face stiff with angers and grievances he'd been recalling.

Anselm sauntered negligently towards him, smiling kindly. Brother Adrian didn't know what to do. He looked wary, then embarrassed, and then almost afraid.

Anselm came right up close, looking into Adrian's face, and with one of his pretty, long-lashed dark eyes, winked.

The reaction was beyond anything he'd have considered possible: Adrian shrieked obscenities and fell writhing to his knees. He tried to pull at Anselm's robe, but Anselm swished decorously away. Adrian crawled after him, screaming that he was going to tear off that garment and show the stinking sin beneath; he scrabbled along the stone floor, he gibbered and finally laughed with fury. But Anselm walked ahead, whisking his skirts to the side in order to avoid the clawing hands. And when he came to the next turning, he scooted around the corner as fast as he could, and went back to his room.

* * *

'Did you provoke him, Anselm?' Francis asked. They were standing outside Frederick's office.

Anselm looked tranquil and he was smiling. 'Brother Adrian provokes himself,' he answered. 'That's his misfortune. It appears to be an exaggerated sense of aggression against others, but actually the main conflict is within.'

'He cracked completely.'

'It may mean that when he comes out, he'll have solved the original trouble.'

'He might not ever come out of it.'

134

Anselm would have liked to say: *It was him or me*. He asked,
'Do you think he was a bad man?'

'Was?'

'We're not sure what he is now. He's just collapsed.'

'Not bad, no.'

'And me? Do you think I'm bad, or morally reprehensible,
or something like that?'

'Of course not. But I do think it's bad that you haven't been
to confession or to Mass, or anything, in so long.'

'I've told you: there's no need. I'm in the care of a higher
power.'

'It's been months.'

'Since the Annunciation, yes.'

'Was it a higher power that struck down Brother Adrian?'

Anselm laughed. 'I love these verbal tennis games,' he
said. 'They're just like theology. This is the way they decide
how many angels can dance on the head of a pin, and get the
exact number, too. Disquisitions and inquisitions. Nobody's
interested in the truth. Look at me, Francis. This is the truth.'

'Anselm, I think you're going about things the wrong way.'

'If you were in my place, would you be scared?'

'I don't know what I'd be.'

'You were always the understanding one. You have a sense
of humanity. But against Frederick's ambitions and neuroses,
you're impotent.'

'I wish you wouldn't talk like this.'

'Francis, who was there to speak up for me against Adrian?
I needed protection against him. Did you or Frederick give
me that? No. You stand there and ask me if I provoked him.'

Thudding and scraping sounds came from beyond the
door. It sounded as if Frederick had begun to move the
furniture.

'Don't feel bad about it,' Anselm added. 'I still like you,
Francis. I just don't like the situation.'

The door opened suddenly. Frederick glared out at them.
'All right, Anselm,' he snapped. 'Come on in.'

'Should I – ?' Francis offered.

135

'You go back to the chapel.' Frederick held the door for Anselm and then swung it away fast so that it slammed. He hurled himself solidly into the best chair. 'Sit down,' he ordered.

Anselm settled himself gingerly on the side of the sofa, with plenty of pillows behind him.

'Anselm, you do realize we can't keep you here?'

'Oh? Isn't the mother of God good enough for your order?'

'It's a question of morality.'

'It always is.'

'Men and women under the same roof. Besides, there's no proof that there was divine intervention.'

'You could say that every woman is the mother of God.'

'You could. I wouldn't. And in your case it isn't even proven how far the womanhood extends.'

'Was the divine aspect proven the first time? I thought they just took her word for it. She told her old husband and he believed it, or said he did.'

'There's a certain amount of feeling in the community that your story is put at a great disadvantage by the absence of, ah, a halo.'

Anselm glanced up, looking at a reproduction of the madonna and child which hadn't been on display the last time he'd been in the room, or at any other time he could remember. It was undoubtedly the cause of the noise he and Francis had heard from outside: it must have taken a long time to get it out from where it had been hidden. The heads of mother and child were each encircled by a band of light like the orbit of a moon around a planet.

'The halo', Anselm said, 'is a symbolic representation of an inner warmth or glow. Fire around the head is supposed to indicate enlightenment of the mind. It isn't peculiar to the Christian tradition.'

'Nevertheless, it is strongly felt that the presence of a halo would be a desirable adjunct to anyone entertaining aspirations to a holy state. It would add authenticity to your claims. Such as they are.'

He had never believed it. Frederick wouldn't countenance anything that wasn't in the books.

'If you doubt me all along the line,' Anselm said, 'what do you think the explanation is?'

'I wouldn't presume to advance a theory as to that. All I know is that the Church is against it.'

'How do you know that?'

For a moment Anselm thought that Frederick would actually break loose and say: *Because the Church is against women.* It seemed to be what he thought; but instead he answered, 'Because it doesn't make sense.'

'What does?'

'It doesn't fit in with scriptural, social, or indeed biological precedence.'

'You think it should have happened to you?'

'Heaven forbid. You don't even seem to understand that in other people's eyes this is a hideous and freakish thing to have occurred.'

'I know that. Oh, yes. Or funny. But not for all of them. A few have been good about it. I expect it's those few that scare you.'

'Scared? The Church has weathered a great many storms over the past centuries.'

'And caused some.'

'It isn't scared.'

'I give up,' Anselm said. 'You won't even think about it, will you? You just push it away. All right – you don't want me here; where do I go? I'll have to live on something, and I won't be able to work when the baby comes.'

'Brother Duncan has given me the name of a reputable nursing home.'

'The arrangement was that I was to go into a place where they'd have all the latest equipment. Either that, or stay here and have an old-fashioned home delivery. Duncan didn't want to risk that.'

'Well, the arrangements have been changed. Brother Duncan now agrees with us that the discretion of the private

137

clinic outweighs the conviviality of a public ward. The medical attention will be in all respects identical.'

Anselm clasped his hands lightly over his bulging front. He knew now what they were going to do to him. First it was William, and then the business with Adrian must have given them a better idea: to put Anselm in a home for the insane. He was sure that that was what they had in mind.

'All right,' he said. He fished around awkwardly for support and lumbered to his feet. Frederick made no move to help. *I hope your nose rots away*, Anselm thought, *and your fingers drop off one by one. I hope you die in pain. I hope it feels like your death lasts longer than your life ever did.*

'Goodbye, Frederick,' he said. 'I hope you think about me sometimes.'

'Of course, Anselm. I don't reproach you.'

'I hope you think about what you've done.'

'I have the welfare of the order at heart, you know that.'

'Horseshit.'

'If that's the way you're going to behave, perhaps you'd better leave now.'

'I'm trying to.' Anselm reached for the doorknob and opened the door. He said, 'And now you can go wash your hands.'

* * *

He pounded on Duncan's door with his fist and opened it himself. The doctor was sitting at his desk, papers in one hand and a ballpoint pen in the other. Anselm closed the door behind him.

'Are those my committal documents?'

'How's that?'

'Don't smile at me, Judas. The whole damn gang of you.'

'Anselm, we're doing our best for you.'

'Going to put me in the loony bin, and my baby too.'

'The child will have the best care imaginable.'

'The best care imaginable is me.'

'An unmarried mother cannot be said to be a person of high moral standards.'

'Then I think you'd better marry me.'

'I thought you didn't like me. Or, so you said.'

'There isn't any choice. You're the last one on the list. William was the one I wanted. And after that, Francis is at least a good man. But he doesn't have any strength left. You're the only one around who can protect me.'

'I see. And why should I?'

'What did he give you, Duncan?'

'I don't know what you mean.'

'Oh yes, you do.'

'It doesn't matter.'

'Then it won't make any difference if you tell me. What was the bribe?'

'They promised me I could go to Africa. Have my own hospital. A crew of novices working under me – everything. All my dreams.'

'That's a lot more than it's worth, unless my story's true. And if it is, then there isn't any price high enough, is there? Do you think they'll keep their word?'

'Now that I think about it, no.'

'Of course not. They've strung you along for so many years now, they know they can do it for ever. All the part of you that could have been your life has become your fantasy world. And your real life has become theirs. It's been going on for years, till you don't have a life of your own any more. You do what they tell you.'

Duncan dropped the pen and papers. 'Go away,' he said.

'And they're telling you: *Get rid of Anselm.* You know what that means. If you have to kill me, they won't care. How much does being a doctor mean to you?'

'It's the way I came to God.'

'And when did you stop believing?'

'Right at the beginning,' Duncan said. 'During the long cold spell when all the old men stayed in their beds.' He looked away and sighed. 'That was before your time. I realized they'd be better in a nursing home, but I also saw how they were degenerating from day to day; how the decay of the body was becoming the decay of the mind. It was a natural progression. And the next stage was for both to come to a stop.'

'Why did you stay?'

'Because it broke me. I used to think I was too good to stay outside. I found out I wasn't good enough to go back. I didn't think it was worthwhile trying to save anybody from anything.'

'Are you going to marry me?'

Duncan's gaze ranged over the shelves where his medical reference books stood, and the filing boxes that held all the case histories of the monastery for the past twelve years. He looked at his framed certificates hanging on the wall, at the small crucifix propped against the one-volume Webster's dictionary; and at Anselm.

'All right,' he said. 'Get ready to leave tonight. I'll come to your door at eleven.'

*   *   *

They drove all night, Duncan behind the wheel. Anselm fell asleep and woke to hear the doctor talking to himself.

'Silly', Duncan muttered, 'to worry about them being able to stop me getting to Africa. I see the light now. The case of my career. Lucky I've taken a lot of notes.'

They were driving along a straight desert road at a speed of nearly ninety miles an hour.

'Slow down,' Anselm ordered. When Duncan didn't seem to hear, he shouted, 'Slow down, I said. We're going too fast.'

The doctor eased his foot from the pedal. 'I was thinking about something else,' he said.

'Think about the road.'

Anselm went back to sleep and woke once more to find that they were driving very fast again. It kept happening all through the night. Towards morning he was exhausted and beginning to feel cramping pains. They came to a place in the road where he could see slopes of green meadows ahead and a stream beyond.

140

'Stop the car,' he said.

'We've got to get as far away as possible.'

'I've got to go to the bathroom. Now.'

Duncan pulled over to the side.

They were in the middle of an empty landscape. It was just before daybreak; everything lay quiet in the grey light.

Anselm got out. He nearly fell. The pains were growing worse. He staggered across the field towards the stream. He was frightened. He thought he might be dying or that the baby could have been hurt, or that he had started to bleed. And he remembered how Duncan had said that as a student he used to have a foetus in a bottle and had studied it.

It would be better, he thought, to drown himself in the river straight away.

'Come back,' Duncan called after him, but Anselm struggled forward against the surging pain that threw him from side to side.

He was coming to the bank of the stream just as Duncan caught up with him and grabbed him by the elbow. Anselm beat back with his free hand, screaming.

'It's all right, Anselm – I'm a doctor,' Duncan shouted at him.

'Let me go – '

'Cut it out. Stop that, or I'll give you an injection.'

'Bastard!' Anselm shrieked. He kicked and twisted. The doctor let go, dropped to the ground and took a tight grip on Anselm's knees. Anselm fought. He dragged himself forward with the doctor hanging on. The dawn began to break around them. He tried with all his strength to gain the bank. He screamed for help until at last, impelled on the tide of his urgency, he reached the water's edge.

The sky opened. Brightness rained down on him. And he was carried along quickly, borne up and up and forward in the sweeping rush of the power he'd been searching for all his life: the wave that goes on for ever.

141